PRAISE FOR *HUNGER WINTER*

I read this book with great interest. I would love to encourage everyone to read this book. *Hunger Winter* succeeds in describing a very realistic picture of the situation in the Netherlands when the country was in a very difficult time. It is important that people learn about the horrors of that awful period in time and realize that— unfortunately—in many places around the world people are still at each other's throats. Hence, it is important that each of us ask ourselves, What will I do in such a situation?

FRITS NIEUWSTRATEN, DIRECTOR, CORRIE TEN BOOM HOUSE FOUNDATION

As someone who has been fascinated by World War II ever since I was a child, *Hunger Winter* is a realistic depiction of what life could very well have been like for children like Dirk and Anna during some of the darkest days the Netherlands has ever known. Rob Currie's ability to create and sustain a narrative that will keep you on the edge of your seat is truly amazing! I highly recommend this powerful and riveting story to *all* readers, young and old alike!

C. DAVID BALIK, ED.D., VICE PRESIDENT USA, ACSI

A well-researched novel on a topic that has rarely been explored in books for young people.

MARSHA FORCHUK SKRYPUCH, AUTHOR OF *MAKING BOMBS FOR HITLER*

I could not put this down. From the first words I felt as if I was in the same grip of fear that Dirk and Anna were facing. Each chapter built a crescendo of anticipation in the hopes of finding their sister and father. This is an excellent work in the historical-fiction genre.

Join thirteen-year-old Dirk Ingelse as he takes readers on his fast-paced journey of being captured by Nazi soldiers, escaping, then avoiding their grasp. Not only does he search for his and his younger sister's safety, but he seeks answers to some tough life questions. Set in the Netherlands at the height of the Dutch Resistance during World War II, this book promises any middle school student an enjoyable and educational read.

Hunger Winter is an exciting tale with great action and wonderfully likable characters. Kids will enjoy the suspense and action while being inspired by its values of love, loyalty, and courage.

From the opening chapter, I found myself caught up in the plight of Dirk and Anna. Join this pair of siblings in their search for safety, their flight for freedom, and their fight for faith as they navigate a maze of Nazi soldiers, collaborators, and kidnappers.

CARL KOHNS, FIFTH-GRADE TEACHER, AVENAL ELEMENTARY SCHOOL, AVENAL, CA

The novel connects the reader to the emotional journey of Dirk, who is an adolescent struggling with challenge after challenge in Nazi German-occupied Europe. The reader is gripped with anticipation as Dirk overcomes one obstacle only to find himself facing an even more daunting situation. Dirk's struggles are realistic and keep the reader from putting the book down.

JOSH HORTON, SIXTH- TO EIGHTH-GRADE ELA AND SOCIAL STUDIES TEACHER, HAMPSHIRE MIDDLE SCHOOL, HAMPSHIRE, IL

This book will definitely be of interest to many. It will grab the attention of those who enjoy an action story as well as those with an interest in Dutch history. Young people will enjoy reading the story of Dirk and Anna to find out how their story unfolds.

TRIXINE TAHTINEN, DIRECTOR OF THE OOSTBURG PUBLIC LIBRARY, OOSTBURG, WI

A realistic portrayal about the riveting events that the Dutch children and adults went through during World War II, *Hunger Winter* will compel you to keep reading. The struggle that faces Dirk and his little sister, Anna, leaves readers on the edge of their seats. Narrowly escaping all the negatives that go along with the war, Dirk and

Anna are unforgettable characters that will leave a lasting and powerful presence in your mind. This enthralling story will grab both young adults and children alike and teach them all about the Netherlands' darkest days during World War II.

KRISTIN NOACK, EIGHTH-GRADE ENGLISH AND LANGUAGE ARTS TEACHER, SHELDON MIDDLE SCHOOL, SHELDON, IA

I pride myself on understanding what early adolescents will like. And believe me, they will like this book! I wish I would have had this book when I was teaching middle school history. Rob Currie gives readers authentic history, armchair-gripping excitement and suspense, as well as meaningful values and lessons. I heartily recommend *Hunger Winter* and already have some school libraries in mind where I would like to send it. If you have children or grandchildren in this age bracket (grades 4–8), I heartily recommend buying this book for them or even reading it together as a family reading time.

MARILOU LONG, FOUNDER/CHANCELLOR OF WILLIAM CAREY ACADEMY

Heroes are usually born during times of war, and during those hardships we truly see the human spirit come alive for good, and we cheer when good triumphs. This is one of those books. You'll get wrapped up in the story of young Dirk and his family from page one. . . . All readers will be caught up in the wonder of the journey this brother and sister must endure in the midst of a world gone terribly wrong. *Hunger Winter* is a treasure of truth and light, courage and strength. Enjoy!

MICHELLE HILL, HOST/PRODUCER OF FAMILYLIFE THIS WEEK

This is a fine book! I can't wait to share it with my librarian friends and young readers in my own family. Set in 1944, this story of a Dutch family during the German occupation will engage readers with riveting action, Dutch traditions, danger, loyalty, and faith. Bravo to author Rob Currie. I loved it all—every word and every layer.

LOUISE BORDEN, AUTHOR OF *SKI SOLDIER: A WORLD WAR II BIOGRAPHY*

THE NETHERLANDS

AMSTERDAM

Scheveningen

Rotterdam

Doorwerth Oosterbeek
Arnhem

Driel
Nijmegen

THE JOURNEYS

Scheveningen

Rotterdam

AMSTERDAM

Doorwerth Oosterbeek
Arnhem

Driel

Nijmegen

- - - - - **Dirk and Anna**
- - - - - **Els**

WESTERN EUROPE

NORTH

SEA

SCOTLAND

●Edinburg

UNITED

KINGDOM

IRELAND

DUBLIN

ENGLAND

□ LONDON

NETHERLANDS

□ASTERDAM

BERLIN □

PRUSSEL □

BELGIUM

LUXEMBOURG

GERMANY

PRAGUE

□

CZECH REP.

PARIS

□

FRANCE

BERNE

□

SWITZ.

□ LIECHTENSTEIN

VIENNA □

AUSTRIA

MEDITERRANEAN SEA

HUNGER WINTER

HUNGER WINTER

A WWII NOVEL

R O B C U R R I E

Tyndale House Publishers
Carol Stream, Illinois

Visit Tyndale's website for kids at tyndale.com/kids.

Visit the author online at robcurrieauthor.com.

TYNDALE and Tyndale's quill logo are registered trademarks of Tyndale House Publishers.

Hunger Winter: A World War II Novel

Author photograph by Pat Hargis. Used with permission.

Designed by Daniel Farrell

Edited by Sarah Rubio

Published in association with the literary agency of The Steve Laube Agency.

Hunger Winter is a work of fiction. Where real people, events, establishments, organizations, or locales appear, they are used fictitiously. All other elements of the novel are drawn from the author's imagination.

For manufacturing information regarding this product, please call 1-800-323-9400.

For information about special discounts for bulk purchases, please contact Tyndale House Publishers at csresponse@tyndale.com, or call 1-800-323-9400.

Half of the author's royalties will go to support Compassion International, an organization that gives food, medical care, education, and hope to children in poverty around the world. For more information, visit www.compassion.com.

Library of Congress Cataloging-in-Publication Data

Names: Currie, Rob (Robert Bruce), author.
Title: Hunger winter : a World War II novel / Rob Currie.
Description: Carol Stream, Illinois : Tyndale House Publishers, 2020. |
    LCCN 2019039438 (print) | LCCN 2019039439 (ebook) |
    ISBN 9781496440341 (hardcover) | ISBN 9781496440358 (trade paperback) |
    ISBN 9781496440365 (kindle edition) | ISBN 9781496440372 (epub) |
    ISBN 9781496440389 (epub)
Subjects: LCSH: World War, 1939-1945—Netherlands—Juvenile fiction. |
    World War, 1939-1945—Underground movements—Netherlands—Juvenile fiction. |
    Netherlands—History—German occupation, 1940-1945—Juvenile fiction. |
    CYAC: World War, 1939-1945—Netherlands--Fiction. | World War, 1939-1945—
    Underground movements—Fiction. | Brothers and sisters—Fiction. | Netherlands—
    History—German occupation, 1940-1945—Fiction.
Classification: LCC PZ7.1.C8649 Hun 2020 (print) | LCC PZ7.1.C8649
    (ebook) | DDC [Fic]—dc23
LC record available at https://lccn.loc.gov/2019039438
LC ebook record available at https://lccn.loc.gov/2019039439

Printed in the United States of America

26 25 24 23 22 21 20
7   6   5   4   3   2

stain ———— damage to p.165 made prior to 1/31/22 noted by LMP

I dedicate this book with love to Kay Currie,

who is my bride and joy.

Grant that I may remain brave,
Your servant for always,
And may defeat the tyranny.
Which pierces my heart.

THE DUTCH NATIONAL ANTHEM

The weeks before us will be the most difficult in the existence of our nation.

RADIO ORANJE

[The Dutch people] have been called on to endure sufferings probably worse
than those so far inflicted on any other country in Western Europe.

THE TIMES (LONDON)

CHAPTER ONE

OOSTERBEEK, NETHERLANDS
NOVEMBER 11, 1944

BAM! BAM! BAM!

Dirk Ingelse's eyes flew open, and he raised his head off the pillow. Who could be knocking on the front door? *Gestapo?* His insides turned to ice.

The pounding resumed, the sound carrying easily up the stairs into Dirk's bedroom. It didn't sound like the rap of knuckles—it was more like the thumping of an angry fist. *Or the butt of a rifle.*

It had to be the Gestapo. They had been doing more raids lately, and they often came at night. Who else would pummel the front door of the Ingelses' farmhouse in the middle of the night and risk getting arrested?

Dirk rolled out of bed and crept to his bedroom window. Easing the curtain open just a bit, he kept his face away from the window, like Papa had taught him. He couldn't

1

see a vehicle. *But what if they hid their car?* Dirk's right hand shook.

He couldn't hide. They would tear the place apart to find him. And he couldn't run—they would have the place surrounded. He'd heard stories. His right hand shook harder. It had been doing that a lot ever since—

The assault on the door resumed, even louder this time. "Open up!" growled a deep voice.

Dirk turned from the window and crept down the stairs. "I'll peek outside," he said under his breath. "If it's the Gestapo, I'll say I have to grab the key to let them in." He ran his fingers through his short blond hair. "Then I'll dash through the house and burst out the back." They would catch him for sure, but maybe they would leave his little sister alone.

The banging got faster. "Open up, Dirk!" the voice demanded above the battering being inflicted on the door.

Have the Gestapo come because of Papa? Have they arrested him?

How long would they wait before they broke into the house? Dirk scurried into the kitchen and grabbed a sharp knife. Weighing about forty-eight kilograms and standing a little over one and a half meters tall, he was average weight and a bit tall for his age, but if the Germans thought they would capture him easily, they were dealing with the wrong thirteen-year-old boy. Waving the knife would keep them back so he could sprint out the rear of the house. *And lead them away from Anna.* He edged toward the window closest to the front door.

Dirk swallowed hard and squeezed the knife handle harder. He pushed the curtain aside a few centimeters, gasped, fumbled with the lock, and swung the door open.

"Mr. van Nort!"

Why would his neighbor leave his farm at this hour of the night to come here?

Mr. van Nort hurried in, looked back at the street, and closed the door behind him. His chest heaved.

Dirk stared at the barrel-chested man, who took off his hat and fingered it nervously. "How did you—?"

"I ran."

That has to be two kilometers!

"I had to come right away to warn you."

Dirk gulped. Mr. van Nort stared at the knife.

"Oh." Dirk relaxed his hand, and the knife clattered to the floor. "I thought—"

"The Gestapo took Els," Mr. van Nort said.

"No!" Dirk slammed his hand on the table. "Why?" But he knew why.

Mr. van Nort looked at him sadly. "The Nazis will do anything to find your father."

Even torture my eighteen-year-old sister. "But Els would rather spit in their faces than tell them anything. Especially about Papa."

Mr. van Nort shook his head. "They are animals, and they can force anyone to talk. One man held out for fifteen days before spilling secrets." He stared at the floor. "The next day he died from his injuries."

Dirk grabbed the back of a chair and forced himself to

swallow a sudden sour taste in his mouth. "How did they capture Els?"

"I came as soon as it happened. Els left our house, and I heard a scream a few moments later," Mr. van Nort said.

Dirk squeezed his eyes shut, his stomach twisting.

"I ran to the window." The neighbor grimaced. "She did her best to fight them off, but there were too many of them."

Dirk put his head in his hands. "Why was she at your house in the middle of the night?"

"You've got to leave," Mr. van Nort said.

"She helps the Resistance, doesn't she? And that means you do too."

Mr. van Nort held up a finger. "If Els doesn't talk right away, they'll come here for you and your little sister. That's how they work."

The room swam before Dirk's eyes. "We'll go to Tante Cora's house in Doorwerth."

"But there's no food in the cities," Mr. van Nort said. "Ever since the Germans—"

"I know. But that's where Els told me to go if anything ever happened to her."

"Take as much food as you can carry." Mr. van Nort looked through the window at the street, then back at Dirk. "You need to leave right away. They'll be coming for you, son. Take Anna and go. Now!"

CHAPTER TWO

AFTER MR. VAN NORT LEFT, Dirk's mind raced. *What are the Nazis doing to Els?* But he couldn't do anything for Els right now, and he had to get moving right away to save Anna. If he and Anna found Papa, then Papa would rescue Els. Dirk snatched two coats from the front closet, dropped them on a nearby chair, and flew up the stairs. In his bedroom, he threw on clothes over his pajamas for extra warmth.

How soon would the Gestapo come? In an hour? Fifteen minutes? A car with its lights on approached the house. He peered outside. *No!*

Dirk's muscles tensed, and his eyes flitted between the approaching car and the long driveway which led to the farmhouse. *Should have kept the knife with me.* His breathing became more rapid. If he ran down the stairs right now, he might dash out the back door before they surrounded the house and draw them away from Anna.

But the car passed the farmhouse.

The next one could be coming for me. With fresh urgency,

Dirk rushed to his dresser, jerked open a drawer, grabbed a gray stone shaped like an extra-large coin, and jammed it into his pocket. He rushed into Anna's room, grabbed the first clothes he saw, and shoved them into a bag next to her dresser, pushing them in so hard he ripped a seam.

Anna's doll lay on the bed next to her. But he couldn't carry Anna, food, and the doll. He reached over his six-year-old sister, untied the orange ribbon in the doll's hair, and crammed the colorful strand in his pocket.

"Anna." He shook her shoulder. "We have to go to Tante Cora's."

Her eyelids fluttered. "Huh?"

"It's time to go."

"Why?"

How could he tell his little sister that the Gestapo had hunted down Els and wanted them next? "It'll be all right. Tante Cora will take care of us." Anna's limp body resisted his effort to sit her up. "And we'll play a game on the way. We won't let anyone see or hear us. It'll be like hide-and-go-seek at Oma and Opa's."

"I love Oma and Opa," she said, still half asleep.

"Yes. And they love their grandchildren, too."

Anna's long blonde hair swung forward when Dirk sat her up on the bed to slide clothes on over her pajamas. He scooped her up and hurried down to the kitchen. While she dozed on a chair, he yanked open a cupboard. He stuffed a half dozen potatoes into his pockets, shoved a loaf of bread under his shirt, and tossed a dozen apples into a bag. *Wish I could carry more.* Dirk threw on his coat and helped Anna with hers but only took time to fasten a few buttons on each jacket. He grabbed the bag of clothes, slung the bag of apples over his shoulder, and lifted Anna in his arms, but she was heavier than he expected. *Uh-oh.* He shifted her onto his back, and she leaned into him.

"We're going to play the quiet game now. You can go back to sleep."

"Uh-huh," she murmured.

Dirk scurried away from the house, his muscles taut, looking left and right like radar scanning for enemy aircraft. The moon provided enough light for him to see. Papa would know how to keep from being spotted. *But Papa isn't here. It's up to me.*

At the edge of their farm, they passed a white birch tree, Mama's favorite, but Dirk couldn't bear to look at it. It brought back too many memories. His voice cracked as he said softly, "I'll protect Anna, Mama. I promise."

He glanced back and suddenly regretted his strategy. He'd chosen the most direct route to Doorwerth. But the road threaded through farm country, with few places to hide if someone approached. What if a dog barked or if one sleepless person looked out the window? Car headlights would be obvious from a distance, but what if the Gestapo rode swift and silent on bicycles? Though the Dutch rode bikes more than the Germans, if anyone was out on a bike after curfew, it would be the Nazis. Dirk's chest tightened. And what if they raided his home and then searched the roads for him? It'd be easy for them to catch him when he was carrying Anna. He frowned.

Also, this road was parallel to the train tracks. The Germans moved troops at night by train to be less visible to Allied planes. What if just one soldier on a passing train saw two children out this late after curfew?

Three more kilometers to Tante Cora's. That would be a lot of time out in the open. A patrol would arrest him for being out at night even if they didn't know his papa was Hans Ingelse.

That wasn't all. His arms and legs were rapidly tiring from carrying Anna on his back. He wouldn't be able to carry her all the way to Tante Cora's. He needed a place for them to hide and rest overnight. But where? They'd already scurried past several farms of people he didn't know if he could trust and one who *definitely* couldn't be trusted.

Dirk bit his lower lip, and his right hand started trembling again.

"Don't go out after dark." Dirk could hear Papa's words as if he had said them yesterday, though it had been a few years earlier, when the Germans started cracking down after the Dutch went on strike. "If the Germans see you out at night, they'll bring you in for questioning, and maybe more than that." He had put both hands on Dirk's shoulders. "Go out during the day—act like you're running an errand—and no one will notice you. You're under the cover of daylight." *I miss you, Papa.*

The Germans would *not* catch them. He would outsmart the Nazis by finding a hiding place. But he saw nothing along the sides of the road that would conceal two fugitive children.

A few minutes later the road turned west and away from

the railroad tracks, now following the Nederrijn River. But that brought a new risk. If Anna woke and cried, the sound would carry over flat ground to any German barges passing in the night. Dirk took a long, slow breath and tried to calm himself a bit.

Where could they hide? The route was familiar from previous trips to visit Tante Cora, but he'd never been looking in desperation for a place to take cover. He searched his memory for a place of concealment along the road. *Wait. I think there might be—* His strides lengthened, and his pace increased until his eyes confirmed what his memory had told him.

Up ahead a fifteen-meter evergreen grew on the side of the road. Dirk slowed his pace and studied the lower branches, which hung low to the ground. He nodded. When they reached the tree, he gently set Anna down.

"Crawl under there," he said, lifting the lowest branch. He eased her to her hands and knees. She was groggy and barely awake, but with Dirk's help, she made her way under the cover of the branches. His right hand quieted. When they lay down, their coats and body heat counteracted the cool November night air.

Lying on his back, Dirk looked up in the dark at the canopy of branches and needles. What was the Gestapo doing right now to torment Els? She was one of the strongest-willed people he knew, but how would she do in the hands of the Nazis? His tears flowed. *Focus, Dirk.* He *had* to lead Anna to safety and find Papa. Papa would figure out how to rescue Els.

So much had happened in such a short time. When Mama died two months before, Els withdrew from university to come home and work to pay the bills for the family. But she was gone a lot, so Anna's care fell to Dirk, as if the suddenness of Papa's departure and the shock of Mama's death weren't enough. Dirk had assumed Papa would come back when Mama died, but Els had told him Papa couldn't because home would be the first place the Nazis would look for him. Dirk put his hands to his eyes, but that didn't stop the tears. And then there was the hardest thing of all—the secret he didn't dare tell anyone.

Dirk tossed and turned. "Good night, Papa, wherever you are," he whispered. Tired as he was, he lay awake for a long time waiting for slumber and for the cover of daylight.

CHAPTER THREE

GESTAPO INTERROGATION CENTER
OOSTERBEEK

ELS HAD FOUGHT HARD to avoid capture outside the van Norts' home, but the half-dozen attackers were bigger, stronger, and meaner. Her mind and emotions reeled from the suddenness and brutality of the attack. She'd been told about arrests, but the warnings hadn't captured the emotional gut punch of the experience. Those Nazi thugs had yanked her hands behind her back, tied them, and stuffed her into the back seat of their car. She felt like a bruised piece of fruit as they drove her to the Gestapo interrogation center.

As she jostled around on the seat of the car, a memory in the back of her brain clamored through the pain for her attention. But what was it? Every muscle and joint screamed in agony, making it impossible to focus. But she knew she had to. Her mind grasped for the memory at the edge of her awareness, like a desperate swimmer at night who flails to reach a rescue line but can't see it in the dark ocean water.

The Gestapo car turned toward downtown Oosterbeek and would be at the headquarters soon. Els felt on the verge of recall. Papa had said something about being captured. *But what?* She bit her lower lip.

The car drove over a large bump. The jarring shot bolts of pain through her aching arms and legs, and she groaned through gritted teeth. Why hadn't she paid more attention to what Papa had said? But she'd been so sure the Gestapo would never catch her. She shook her head. What had he told her?

Wait! It was something about the first day of capture. "If they arrest you," he had said—but there was more. She scrunched her eyes shut, willing the memory to show itself. Then it flashed. "If they bring you in for questioning, don't tell them anything for the first day and night." She took a quick breath. That was it! Papa had gone on to explain that if she could hold out that long, it would give others in the Resistance time to relocate. But he had added, "The Nazis know this too, and they will do anything to make you talk right away." Els swallowed hard.

The car stopped. As they muscled her out of the vehicle and into a jail cell, her injuries roared in anguish. The cell wasn't much longer than the old dining table at home. Now she sat and waited, knowing that any minute they'd start in on her. Moans and screams from the interrogation rooms drifted down the hallway to Els's ears. Dutch citizens often complained that Gestapo headquarters played radio music too loud. The Resistance knew this was to drown out the screams of torture, but that music was pumped outside. Inside the building, there was no music—only the cries of brutalized Dutch citizens.

Els slumped on a thin, tattered mattress as she faced the cell door with no handle on the inside. Even though it was the middle of the night, a light blazed overhead. A guard looked in frequently through the peephole in the door. She tried to think of any other advice she'd been given about this situation. But this was real life, and anything could happen now. *Anything.*

Back when the Germans invaded, Els's heart had swelled with pride at her parents' roles in the Resistance, and she'd joined in the effort too. Only thirteen years old at the time, she began by stealing pieces of chalk from school and drawing a large *V*, a common Resistance symbol, on buildings in town. As she got older, she and her friends set fire to the food for the German horses and pried up railroad timbers to derail German trains. When Allied pilots got shot down, Els led them to safe places to stay. Out at night, she excelled at slinking from doorway to doorway to escape detection. The fact that many Dutch were afraid to fight back made these acts of defiance more appealing and thrilling.

Her cell door flew open. A soldier stormed in and yanked her to her feet. She yelped in pain as he hustled her to an office. "*Sitz dich*," he barked, jabbing an index finger toward a chair. Els sat, facing a grim-faced interrogator. He was tall, thin, and bald. His nose had a slight hook to it, like an eagle's beak. He pushed his face close to Els's. "Where is your father? Where does he hide the Jews?" he demanded.

Els's eyes grew wide. This man had just revealed that Papa was alive, and the Nazis didn't know where he was. That was great news! She sat up straight, folded her arms in front of her, and looked the interrogator in the eye. He surged even closer to her, his nose just a few centimeters from hers. "Where is your father? Where does he hide the Jews? Tell me *now*." The veins in his neck bulged as he spat out the words.

"I don't know."

He followed with a barrage of questions. "When was the last time you saw your father? Who was with you? Were you at your home? What time of day was it? What was he wearing? What did you talk about?"

Noting the man's skill in using verbal variety in trying to pry information from her, Els chose a parallel strategy of varying her responses. She alternated "I don't know" with "Papa never told me" and "I don't remember." Sometimes she gave no response, as if the man did not deserve a reply.

"You sit there, as I think you Dutch say it, with your mouth full of teeth," he said as he glared at her.

"I'm not speechless," Els shot back. "I'm just not talking to you."

The rapid-fire questioning continued without results for about two hours. Then the man abruptly stood and left the room.

Fatigue washed over Els. She closed her eyes and slouched in her chair. Her breathing slowed.

Moments later, Els started up as a second interrogator burst into the room. A short man, he had black hair with a few flecks of gray, and gold wire-rimmed glasses. Whereas the first questioner had looked her in the eye at close range, this one roved the room, walking around Els like a predator circling his prey. *Or a python coiling around a victim.* "You will tell us where your father is, or you shall leave us no choice but to take harsher methods." The other man had screamed at her. This man spoke at normal volume but with an edge to his voice. *Like a snake's hiss.*

Els stared at the interrogator, making an effort to keep her face blank.

"You have a younger brother and sister," he said from behind her.

Even the Gestapo wouldn't stoop to harming kids, would they? Els shifted in her chair.

The interrogator stepped in front of her and bent to her eye level. "They fled your home, but we know where they're going."

He *had* to be bluffing. The Nazis were masters of terror and lying, and this had to be one more example. He fixed his eyes on hers, his gaze burning. Didn't this man ever blink?

"It would be a shame if anything were to happen to your brother and sister."

What did he mean by that?

"We *will* capture your father. The only question is if you are wise enough to give us the information we need so nothing happens to Dirk and Anna. We would give you plenty of food ration cards." He reached into his pocket, pulled out a stack of cards, and fanned them out in his hand, like playing cards.

"I know what ration cards look like. I'm not stupid," Els

said. If they were so sure about capturing Papa, why did they need any information from her?

"The level of your intelligence remains to be seen." He laid the cards on the table in a triumphant flourish, like a victorious card player in a game-winning move. "Tell us about your father, and you could have all these cards," he said. "You would, of course, be released so you could care for your brother and sister."

If she took those, she'd be no better than all the Dutch who collaborated with the enemy! She shoved the ration cards off the table with both hands. They scattered on the floor like autumn leaves.

Els sat more erect. "I don't know where my father is."

"Then tell me where he liked to go and the names of his friends. Tell me where he takes the Jews after they leave your farm." He paused. "Dirk is thirteen, and Anna is only six. Do you have any idea what prison would do to a six-year-old?"

A chilling thought flashed through Els's mind. Dirk knew that if anything happened to her, he had to take Anna to Tante Cora's. But what if no one had informed Dirk of Els's capture? What if the Gestapo swooped in and captured her unsuspecting siblings? These questions gnawed at her like a swarm of rats which chew the only rope holding a ship to the dock during a storm.

Papa was right. In the first twenty-four hours the Gestapo would do anything to get information out of her. *Anything.*

"Tell me something about your father!" the Nazi shouted directly in her ear.

She flinched. "I won't tell you anything about Papa," she said in an even tone.

"You will regret saying that to me. More than you can imagine." He stalked out of the room.

Moments later, a third interrogator entered. Unlike the previous man, he came in slowly and closed the door behind him quietly. He was tall and broad shouldered, perhaps thirty years old, with brown hair and very intense brown eyes. In one arm he cradled a black cat and with the other, he stroked its back. Els blinked several times. Since when did Nazi henchmen show any form of humanity?

"Hello, Els," the man said in a soft voice as he sat. He looked to weigh more than ninety kilograms, very muscular. "I am Captain Johann Adler. This is Max." He nodded at the cat. What was this man up to? The soft voice didn't fit the fierce physique. Silently he ran his hand in long, slow strokes over Max's back, and in return the cat purred. This continued for a minute or so.

This man seemed so different from the first two questioners, and nothing in her Resistance training had prepared Els for anything like this. She studied his facial expression for clues and slid her chair a few centimeters away from him. She had to be ready for anything.

Adler moved toward the door and opened it. "Guard," he called. He handed the cat to the guard, and in return received a glass of water.

He looked at Els. "I thought you might be thirsty." He sat down and slid the glass of water across to her.

What was the water for? The Gestapo never showed any kindness, so there had to be something else going on here. *Something nasty.* Els looked at the glass, keeping her facial expression unchanged.

"Go ahead," he said, his voice gentle.

Something about the way he said it unnerved her. She looked at him for a long time before, with a trembling hand, she reached for the glass and raised it to her nose. After several short sniffs, she opened her mouth to drink.

In a flash Adler swung his hand. The force of the blow turned her head and knocked the glass to the other side of the room, where it shattered and sprayed water around the cell. The palm of his hand had smacked her cheek so hard it burned, but that was nothing compared to the surging blaze of her anger.

He shot to his feet. "Now you will tell me where your father is!" he shouted.

"I won't tell you anything." Outrage at this monster's cruelty pushed out the shivers of fear she'd felt moments before, the way a raging forest fire overpowers chilly morning air.

Adler crossed his arms. "You are brave, but bravery with no chance of success is only foolishness. In the end, everyone talks." With the heel of his boot, he crushed a piece of glass and slowly ground it into the cement floor, keeping his eyes fixed on hers. "Everyone."

Adler swept from the room. A guard hurried Els down the hall to her prison cell, shoved her inside, and clanged the door shut behind her.

After some time, the flames of Els's anger slowly died down

into embers of determination. From now on, no matter what the moffen did, she would tell them nothing.

She spotted a pebble which had worked itself loose from the concrete wall. *That's it!* If the Nazis were howling winds and crashing waves, then she would be stone. She would turn her heart to stone—hard, feeling nothing, saying nothing. She grasped the pebble tight in her fist and held it to her chest as she lay down on her skinny mattress. *A heart of stone.* Els closed her eyes and waited for sleep.

CHAPTER FOUR

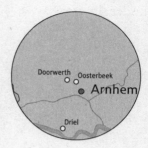

ON THE ROAD TO DOORWERTH
NOVEMBER 12

SQUEAKING NOISES woke Dirk. *Huh?* He crawled quietly away from the evergreen trunk, then raised a branch and peered toward the street. A steady line of bicyclists pedaled past. Other passersby included a teenage boy pulling a wagon and a nun pushing a baby carriage. These people had grabbed whatever they could find that had wheels. They were starving city dwellers going to the farms to trade for food. People like them had come many times to his family's farm. *Until yesterday.*

Behind him, Anna stirred. "Where are we? Why aren't we at home?" Her lower lip quivered.

"We're going to Tante Cora's." He fastened a button on her coat. "Remember? I told you last night."

"Where is Els?" Her blue eyes searched his face.

Of course she would ask questions. Ever since Mama died she had asked many questions, and with Els gone so much, it had fallen to Dirk to answer them.

"Oh, uh . . ." He coughed a few times. "Els is busy, but she'll come when she can. We need to go, but I bet you're hungry. You want an apple?"

"Uh-huh." They crawled out from under the tree.

"Eat it slowly," Dirk said.

"Why?"

He guided her toward the street. "It'll fill you up more if you eat it slowly."

"Oh." She nibbled her apple. A few more cyclists passed by on the road. "Where are those people going?"

When Mama died, Els was away at university and Papa was gone, so Dirk had to tell Anna about Mama's death. Still in shock from finding Mama's body, he couldn't remember the words he'd used, but her reaction was etched in his mind.

"No, no, no, no!" she had cried, shaking her head emphatically from side to side. "Mama's not dead!" She'd pulled away from Dirk and dashed toward their parents' bedroom. Dirk ran after her and found her standing frozen in the room that was as empty as Dirk's heart felt. Her body quivered and then convulsed with grief. Dirk turned away, unable to bear the burden of both his sorrow and hers. Then Anna pushed past him and shot up the stairs, shouting, "Mama's not dead!" before taking refuge in her bedroom, slamming the door behind her.

It was true the apple would fill her up more if she ate it slowly, but there was no way he would tell her about the starving people in the cities. *Or that we'll soon be out of food too.* When they reached the road, he studied it in both directions.

"Why are we going to Tante Cora's?"

"She's Papa's sister. We need to be with someone we can trust, and she lives a lot closer than Tante Jans."

"That's not what I mean. Why did we have to leave our farm?" she asked between bites.

Dirk cleared his throat. How could he explain to a six-year-old about the Gestapo? If he tried now, she would scream, and people would ask questions. *The wrong people.* "I'll tell you all about it when we get to Tante Cora's," he said, avoiding her eyes.

"Are we going to live with Tante Cora and Oom Steffen?"

"We'll live there for a while, but Oom Steffen isn't there anymore. The moffen took him, remember?"

"The moffen?"

"You know, the Nazis." Dirk sighed. If Anna didn't know the Dutch called Nazis *moffen*, what else didn't she know? The family had tried to shield her as much as possible from the war and the occupation, but things were different now. How could he protect her from the enemy when she knew so little about them? So in addition to keeping a step ahead of the Nazis, getting to Tante Cora's, and finding Papa, it'd also be Dirk's job to tell Anna the truth, a little at a time, about the Nazis. *Great.*

"They took Oom Steffen?" Her face fell.

"He was my favorite uncle too, Anna." He took her hand. "Hey, do you want to play hide-and-go-seek when we're at Tante Cora's?"

"I love playing that at Oma and Opa's," she said.

"We can play it at Tante Cora's too."

"Uh-huh. I always use the same spot at Oma and Opa's, and you never find me."

He smiled. "I guess you're just a really good hider."

"Yeah."

Anna munched her apple and chattered about Tante Cora the whole way to town. As they entered the town, off to the left, in the distance, lay Doorwerth Castle. They couldn't see it clearly, but that was fine by Dirk. He had enough questions from Anna already without the sight of the castle triggering fearful inquiries about it being haunted, like Franz, the bully in Dirk's class, had told some of the younger children.

As they walked toward Tante Cora's neighborhood, Dirk only half listened to what Anna said. Despite it being midmorning, most of the shops were closed and many houses were empty. Their darkened windows looked like the eye sockets of skeleton heads.

Dirk gaped at the abandoned buildings. *Where did all the people go?*

Anna seemed to read his thoughts. "What if we get to Tante Cora's, and she's not there?" she asked.

"She'll be there." But what if the Gestapo was there too, waiting for Dirk and Anna after searching their empty house last night?

"Are you sure?" His sister looked up at him.

"Yes," he said. *I hope.* "Come on. We're almost there."

Across the street and ahead a bit, two soldiers warmed themselves by a barrel fire. One stared at Dirk and Anna, then prodded his partner. Dirk's pulse sped up, but he tried to act casual as they walked past. They just had to make it around the next corner, and then they could run or hide. A minute later, right after they turned the corner, an engine sputtered and started.

"Run!" He tugged Anna's arm, and they sprinted up the steps and through the open doorway of an abandoned house. A few seconds later, a motorcycle rumbled by. It didn't shoot past the house but instead crept by, like the soldiers were looking for something. *Or someone.* He strained to listen. The motorcycle came back, closer and closer, until it stopped in front of the house where Dirk and Anna hid.

"Hurry!" he said. He glanced over his shoulder as they raced to the rear of the house. As the soldiers approached what used to be a home, Dirk and Anna reached the back door. With a finger to his lips, Dirk tried to quiet his breathing. "*Kapitulieren Sie!*" a soldier shouted, his rough voice echoing in the empty house. *He's calling out to us to surrender because he thinks we're here, but he's not sure.*

Anna opened her mouth, but Dirk's hand shot up and covered it. He shook his head and slid his hand from her mouth. *Maybe they'll leave if they don't hear or see anything.* But the army boots thumped closer.

Dirk tested the doorknob at the back of the house. *Locked!* He couldn't see a key or any other way to open it. They were just a few blocks away from Tante Cora's, and he couldn't let them be captured now. He dashed to the nearest window and slid it open. He helped Anna crawl through it, then followed her and shut the window again as silently as he could. He motioned for Anna to lie down on the ground next to the house, right under the window. The seconds dragged. *Why would soldiers be suspicious of two kids? Did someone tip them off?* Finally, the motorcycle started. Dirk sighed with relief.

They waited a few minutes and then scurried down several alleys until they saw a familiar brown house ahead on the right. Dirk ran to the front door, pulling Anna by the hand, and knocked. No response. He flinched when he heard voices coming behind him, but it turned out to be Dutch people riding by on bicycles. He kept an ear cocked for any vehicles coming as he knocked again. What would he do if the soldiers came by? If the soldiers went on patrols, they could be coming up the street any minute.

Finally the door opened. "Dirk! Anna!"

"Tante Cora!"

Dirk pulled Anna into the house without waiting to be invited in, looking over his shoulder at the street.

"What are you two doing here? Are you all right?" Tante Cora hugged Dirk and Anna. A short woman in her late forties, she had more gray than blonde in her hair now, and even with her coat on, she looked much thinner than the last time they had visited her.

"We need help," Dirk said.

"Oh my. Come in. Come into the kitchen and tell me," she said.

Dirk and Anna sat at the kitchen table. The house felt only a little warmer than the late-autumn morning outside. Tante Cora stood facing them, rubbing her hands together for warmth.

"Tell me what happened," she said.

Dirk looked at Anna. It would break her heart to hear

the truth, but he had to say it. Tante Cora put a hand on his shoulder. "Did something happen to Els?"

His mouth quivered. "Gestapo," he got out.

Tante Cora's mouth dropped open. She reached behind her for a chair and sank into it. "They took her?"

Dirk nodded.

"Oh my, oh my."

Anna looked at her aunt's stricken face and burst into tears. "Nooo!" She threw her arms around Dirk, and he hugged her tight. He wanted to say Els would be all right, but how could he?

Tante Cora shook her head a few times. She got up and hugged both of them, brushing away tears.

"A neighbor said they would come for us next so they could get to Papa," Dirk said, looking at the floor. He lifted his head. "Do you know where Papa is? He'll know how to help Els."

"I'm sorry, but I haven't heard anything."

Dirk's shoulders fell. Anna sobbed in his arms. "I want to go back home," she said.

"Els told me many times that if anything happened to her, we should come here, Anna. That bullet has already passed through the church."

"What?" she asked, sniffling.

"It's an expression that means this thing has already been talked about and decided upon."

"Oh."

Tante Cora stroked Anna's hair. "You'll be safe here, but I'm almost out of food," she told Dirk.

"We brought some," he said, showing her.

"What do you have?"

"Apples, bread, and potatoes." But how long would this food last for three people?

Tante Cora reached into the bag and pulled out an apple. She turned it over in her hands, held it to her nose, and inhaled. "Ohhh. I haven't had one of these in months." She put it back in the bag and rubbed her hands together. "I'll light a little fire so you can warm up, and I can cook lunch. I'm glad you're here, but I'm surprised Els told you to come." She pointed to the pantry. "The Germans cut off our food two months ago."

"I know," Dirk said, his attention riveted on the nearly bare shelves. Had he made a mistake by bringing Anna here?

"The food you brought will help," Tante Cora said, standing up, "and we'll make the best of things."

She walked over to a metal tube that rested on the stove. Twice as tall as a drinking glass and as wide as a dinner plate, it had a hole near the bottom to insert little pieces of wood. Tante Cora struck a match and held it to the wood until it caught, then she started to slice a potato into small pieces.

When Anna headed to the bathroom, Dirk stepped closer to his aunt. "Where's Heinrich?"

Tante Cora stopped cutting. "Somebody stole him."

"What?! Why would someone steal a dog?"

She set the knife down. "People do desperate things when they're hungry."

"Ohhh." He turned away.

Tante Cora resumed cutting the potato, but more slowly

than before. Dirk looked around the kitchen until Anna returned from the bathroom.

"While you're waiting for the soup to cook, why don't you two play a game?" Tante Cora said. They walked into the living room, where a Sjoelbak board rested on the large table. Dirk was in no mood for a game, but he played anyway. *Maybe it'll help Anna.* They took turns sliding the disks toward targets, and he grunted whenever she made a better shot than he did. Each time it happened, she clapped, jumped up and down, and said, "I'm good at this game!" Tante Cora gave Dirk a knowing smile. Twenty minutes later they returned to the kitchen for lunch.

Dirk should have enjoyed the meal. He was hungry enough, but they had just used two potatoes. At that rate, the food he had brought wouldn't last the week. How would he take care of Anna when the food ran out?

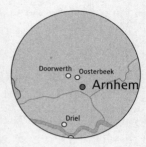

CHAPTER FIVE

DOORWERTH

THAT AFTERNOON as they sat in the kitchen, Tante Cora said, "Dirk, I want you to dig up the tulip bulbs from our front yard before someone else does."

"Why?"

She glanced at Anna, who was in the living room, leaned forward, and lowered her voice. "With three mouths to feed, our food will be gone soon, and we need the tulip bulbs to make soup." She raised her voice. "Anna, you can help me sort clothing scraps. We'll sew them together so my favorite niece and nephew can have more blankets to keep warm." She winked. "You could drape one over your shoulders and call yourself a princess." Anna beamed.

For supper they had apples, bread, and more potato soup. Dirk's stomach still growled after the meal, but he knew they had to make the food last as long as possible, so he didn't complain.

31

That night, Anna shivered under the covers. "I'm cold."

"Come over by me," Dirk said. She hesitated, then dashed across the room, crawled under the covers, and nestled next to him. He pulled the blankets up to her chin and adjusted her pillow. Two minutes later, her breathing became slow and regular.

The next morning, Dirk waited in line with a bucket at the soup kitchen, his breath forming clouds in the cold morning air. He kept his free hand in his pocket and stamped his feet. When he received his portion of soup, he studied it. Tiny bits of vegetable swirled in a broth that looked like gray water. Despite his hunger, the soup didn't smell good, but the steam rising from it warmed his face.

After breakfast, they rested. "We have to save our energy," Tante Cora said.

"Take the wheelbarrow and saw to the park," Tante Cora told Dirk after lunch. "Cut down a small tree. Thanks to the Nazis, we have the unholy trinity—the cold, the dark, and the hunger. But tonight we'll have heat."

At the park, Dirk stopped in front of a small oak tree. After he sawed for twenty minutes, the tree wavered, the trunk crackled, and it hit the ground with a *thump*. Despite his tired arms, he didn't rest. He sawed the trunk into pieces for another half hour and loaded the wood into the wheelbarrow. When he finished, he took a moment to visualize sitting by a fireplace while the wood burned. He held his hands in front of him and warmed them over the imaginary flames.

"*Was ist das?*" a voice said from behind, but it wasn't a friendly greeting. It was more like a growl. Dirk jumped.

When he turned around, three soldiers were behind him. One pulled a pistol from his holster. "*Gib es uns!*" he said and nodded at the wood. Dirk stepped back, raised his hands, and stared at the weapon. *This can't be happening to me!*

An army truck approached. "*Gib es uns!*" the man repeated. With the gun still aimed at him, Dirk loaded the wood into their vehicle. He gritted his teeth but didn't say anything. When the soldiers left, one of them laughed and pointed at him. The moffen weren't satisfied to steal the food and fuel of the Dutch. They wanted to crush their spirit, too.

Dirk trudged back to the house, his insides feeling as empty as the wheelbarrow he pushed. "It's not fair," he said.

Tante Cora put her arm around him. "You're right, but we'll figure out another way to scrounge some wood. At least you're safe."

Anna entered from an adjoining room. She had a blanket wrapped around her, and her teeth chattered. "Where's the wood?"

"The Germans took it," Tante Cora said.

"But you said we'd have a fire tonight." She hurried to the living room and grabbed another blanket. "Why's your house so cold?"

Tante Cora bent down and looked Anna in the eye. "After the invasion, when our country surrendered to the Germans, they were very polite and pretended to be our friends. But when Dutch workers went on strike to protest sending Jews away, things changed. That's when the monkey came out of the sleeve."

"What monkey?" Anna asked.

"It means the Germans' true intentions finally showed, and they treated us a lot worse. And a couple of months ago, when the Dutch train workers went on strike to keep the German army from getting where it wanted to go, the Nazis punished us by cutting off food and fuel."

She adjusted Anna's blanket so that it covered her head like a makeshift hood.

Anna frowned. "Can't we make them give us what we need? I'm cold and I'm hungry."

"Not until the Allies come and kick the Nazis out."

The next morning in the food line, a man told Dirk he'd heard there would be meat in the soup. When Dirk got his bucket filled, there was a bit of meat floating on the top of the broth—a mouse's tail. He dumped the soup on the ground.

"You did the right thing," Tante Cora said when he returned. "But now I need you to go to a farm just outside of town and buy grain." She grabbed a coin out of her purse. "I can spare only one rijksdaalder, but see how much they will give you."

Dirk smiled and adjusted his hat.

"Hurry. We don't want the farmer to run out of food before you get there." She gave him a pillowcase, and he headed for the farm.

As he walked out of town, he saw many people going the same direction. Some walked, but most were on bicycles. He *had* to make up for coming home from the soup kitchen empty-handed. As he got close to the farm, he saw people leaving with full pillowcases or buckets.

When he reached the line for food, more than twenty people stood ahead of him. Was he too late? *Uh-oh.*

"How much are they charging?" he asked the woman ahead of him.

"Two rijksdaalders," she said.

Dirk grimaced, reached in his pocket, and fingered his lone coin. His right hand, which touched the rijksdaalder, shook. His mouth got dry. What if he returned home *again* without any food? How would he explain that to Tante Cora and Anna? By the time he reached the table where a farmer sold the grain, his stomach was twisted in knots. Every person in front of him had paid two rijksdaalders.

"Next," the farmer said.

Dirk stepped into the barn and handed the man the coin, but his words stuck in his throat. When he managed to speak, his voice cracked. "I only have one rijksdaalder."

"Only one rijksdaalder? Hmm." Chatter in the line stopped.

Dirk wrung his hands. "It's for my aunt and my little sister. Please, sir."

"Follow me," the man said with a stern expression, and he walked to a stall. He paused dramatically, filled Dirk's pillowcase to the top, tied it with string, and burst into a big grin.

"That's how we treat a young man with only one rijks-daalder." He tousled Dirk's hair. "Now go on home and be safe."

Dirk's right hand immediately stopped shaking, and he grasped the heavy pillowcase with both hands.

He strode back to town, smiling broadly. If he hadn't been carrying ten kilos of grain, he might have run the whole way. When he arrived, Tante Cora was sitting at the dining room table sewing rags together. She saw Dirk's big bag, dropped her needle and thread, and nearly jumped out of her chair to give him a hug.

"Ohhh! Ohhh! This is wonderful!" She told him that while he carried out his errand, she and Anna had cut down a short tree and brought the wood home.

After supper, with the fire low and the house dark, Tante Cora shared memories of growing up as Papa's big sister. She also told Dutch fairy tales—"The Boy Who Wanted More Cheese" and "The Legend of the Wooden Shoe." She winked when she changed "The Princess with Twenty Petticoats" to "Princess Anna with Twenty Petticoats."

At story time the next night, Anna said, "Make Princess Anna brave, and make her older than Dirk." While they huddled under the blankets, Tante Cora told tales until Anna fell asleep.

"May I ask you something, Tante Cora?" Dirk asked as he adjusted his blanket.

"Of course."

He paused. "How did the Germans catch Oom Steffen?"

"Oh my, oh my."

"If you don't want to talk about it—"

"No. I can get through this. I'm not the only woman who lost her husband that day." She wiped away tears with both hands. "The Germans staged a razzia early in the morning.

Dozens of trucks rumbled into town, and soldiers were everywhere, taking able-bodied men and teenage boys."

"Because they helped the Resistance?"

"No."

"Was it because they hid Jews?"

"No. To work in their factories in Germany." Her lower lip trembled. "The soldiers burst into houses and tore the men right out of their homes."

Dirk pictured the Nazis rounding up the men while their wives wailed and their children clung to them. He cringed. "So they came here and found Oom Steffen?"

Tante Cora shook her head. "He wouldn't hide because he knew each man taken would probably never see his wife and children again." She blew her nose. "He knew the danger, but he made up his mind to alert every family he could. On his way back to our house, a neighbor saw them capture him." She took a shaky breath. "His courage saved many families. But ours was not one of them."

They sat in silence. Tante Cora and Oom Steffen never had children. Dirk wondered if anyone helped his aunt now that she was alone. After Mama died, people brought meals and helped with chores for a couple of weeks, but then they got busy and went back to their own lives.

"I'm sorry for asking you," Dirk said.

After a long silence, she sniffed. "It's all right. It's not the first time I've cried for him, and it won't be the last."

After he went to bed, Dirk lay awake for a long time. How much had the Gestapo tortured Els by this time? He brushed away a tear. He *had* to find Papa so he could set her free. Maybe he would lead a Resistance force to storm the building.

The whole family needed Papa, but Dirk didn't know when they would see him again. *Or if.*

CHAPTER SIX

NOVEMBER 16

BY NINE THE NEXT MORNING the temperature was well above freezing, and there was no wind. After one of Tante Cora's neighbors passed the word about available food at a nearby farm, Dirk grabbed his coat and hat to hike there to trade silverware for eggs, milk, and vegetables.

"I want to go too," Anna said.

Tante Cora opened the curtains which faced the street, and sun streamed into her living room. "That's fine since it's warmer today, and it's less than three kilometers away," she said. "Dirk will watch out for you."

"What do you mean?"

"I just mean it's good to have an older brother or sister to protect you."

"From soldiers?"

"From anything."

"Tante Cora, since you are Papa's older sister, did you ever have to protect him?"

"Yes, a couple of times, Anna."

"Really?" Her eyes brightened.

"That sounds like a good bedtime story for tonight, but you two need to get going now." Tante Cora patted Anna on the arm. "While you're gone, I'll visit my neighbor who just had a baby." She put a homemade blanket and a few packets of tea into a basket and set it by the door.

An hour later Dirk and Anna had almost reached the farm.

"I'm hungry," Anna said.

Dirk looked down at her and stroked her hair. "I know. We're all hungry. But we'll trade for food at the farm."

"But I want something now." She clutched her abdomen.

"Do you want to ride in the wheelbarrow?"

"Uh-huh." He lifted her in.

A few minutes later, she shrieked.

Dirk nearly dropped the wheelbarrow handles. "What's wrong?" He bent over Anna and studied her face.

She scrunched her eyes shut and pointed ahead.

The lifeless body of a middle-aged woman lay by the side of the road. The woman wore a black coat over her dress, and she had no shoes.

"Why is that lady lying there?"

Dirk hesitated. He wanted to keep shielding Anna from the war as much as possible, but she needed to know what the moffen were capable of. "Uhh . . . she probably starved to death." He picked up the wheelbarrow handles and resumed walking. "She probably just ran out of strength and hope and gave up." He managed to keep his voice steady, but how many more times would he have to hide his feelings from Anna?

"Why don't the Germans bury her?"

"They want us to think that resisting the Nazis is hopeless, and they left her there to send a message." He gritted his teeth. "Just don't look until I tell you."

She scrunched her eyes shut.

When they drew even with the body, Dirk took a closer look. The woman's mouth and eyes were open. Did she have a family? How would they find out about her? He shuddered.

"Okay, Anna. You may open your eyes. Do you see the farm up ahead?"

"Uh-huh."

The farmer took their silverware in exchange for a dozen eggs, two liters of milk, and two bags of vegetables. On the way back, his spirits boosted by the amount of food they had received, Dirk waved at the many cyclists who rode past him.

They came back to the place where the dead woman lay. Someone had draped the Dutch tricolor over her body.

"Why did someone put a Dutch flag over that lady?" Anna asked.

Dirk narrowed his eyes. "Because the Nazis aren't the only ones who know how to send a message."

By the time they neared Doorwerth, Dirk's hands were sore and his arms ached from pushing the wheelbarrow, but he kept going. He could rest when they got back to Tante Cora's. What would their aunt say this time when she saw how much food they'd gotten? What would she prepare for dinner, and how good would it smell while it cooked? *And how good will it taste?* His mouth watered.

But five minutes from the house, they turned a corner, and Dirk froze.

One block ahead, German soldiers combed the neighborhood, going from house to house. They dragged a man from his house while his wife pounded on the soldiers with her fists. For an instant, Dirk couldn't move.

"What's happening?" Anna asked.

"A razzia. We're going to get out of here," he whispered, keeping his eyes on the troops.

"I'm scared, Dirk." She reached up to him.

He lifted her out of the wheelbarrow. "Run to the alley," he said. As they dashed in that direction, a convoy of troop carriers lumbered toward them. Soldiers clambered out of the vehicles and ran toward Dirk and Anna.

"*Halt!*"

Anna screamed.

"Keep going," Dirk urged, pulling on her hand, but footsteps pounded closer behind them. If he'd been alone, he might have escaped, but he had to slow his pace to stay with Anna.

Just before he reached the alley, a strong hand grabbed him from behind and spun him around. "*Gehe*," the soldier with the iron grip said, pointing toward the inside of a nearby truck where weeping civilians sat, some with their heads down. Dirk nearly lost his balance but shot his arms out to his sides and managed to stay on his feet. The infantryman grabbed Dirk by both wrists and tugged him toward the truck.

"Dirk!"

He twisted free from his captor's grip. He looked around wildly for Anna only to find she was just three meters away.

"Run, Anna!" *Ohh!* If only she had kept running! But she must have been frozen in fear while Dirk had worked himself free. In the few seconds he'd taken to shake off the kidnappers, more soldiers had closed in.

A soldier ran up to him. "*Schwein!*"

Only the Nazis would deprive someone of food and then have the nerve to call him a pig. Dirk faked one way and darted the other way, but the soldier, eyeing the opening to the alley, stepped in Dirk's path. Eyes flashing anger and teeth bared, the man was a two-legged attack dog.

"Get out of my way!" Dirk yelled.

The soldier surged forward and grabbed a fistful of Dirk's shirt, but he spun away. The German swung a massive backhand at him, but Dirk ducked, lowered his shoulder, and accelerated into his enemy's undefended abdomen. Papa had taught him the best time to make a move is right after your opponent lunges at you because he's off balance.

"Uhh!" the soldier grunted and stumbled backward.

It worked!

A broad-shouldered man two meters tall stepped in Dirk's path and reached for his shoulders.

But thanks to wrestling lessons from Papa, Dirk knew what to do with this Nazi mountain. It was time to start a landslide.

Dirk surged forward, placed a leg behind the man's feet, and pushed his chest with all his strength. The man toppled and landed hard with a muffled groan.

Dirk whirled to find Anna, but another soldier's fist landed solidly on Dirk's mouth, and he tasted blood. He stared at his enemy without flinching, but someone shoved him hard from behind and he fell forward. A big boot slammed onto his back, pinned him to the ground, and forced the air from his lungs. He panicked for a few seconds, gasping. Once he could breathe, he tried to roll out from under the pressure on his back.

"*Nein, Schwein,*" Big Boot said.

Strong hands pulled Dirk's hands behind him, tied them together, and jerked him to his feet.

Anna ran up to Dirk and grabbed the hem of his shirt. Big Boot pointed toward the truck. "*Schnell, Dummkopf.*"

Unaffected by the insult to his intelligence, Dirk freed his arms by twisting out of Big Boot's grasp, but he couldn't fight this many soldiers, especially with his hands tied behind him and Anna clinging. But there was another way! An alley had hiding spots, and he knew this part of town well from previous visits to Tante Cora. "Anna! Hold onto me!" He darted toward a gap between the soldiers. The alley was only meters away.

"*Ergreift sie!*" a voice shouted behind them. Heavy feet pounded.

Just before they reached the alley, Dirk felt Anna's hands pull away from his shirt, ripping the cloth. She screamed.

"No!" Dirk looked back and saw that a burly soldier was carrying Anna toward the truck.

"Dirk!" she shrieked, reaching for him. She kicked her legs against her captor's chest, but they had no effect.

Dirk dashed toward the man. "Let her go!"

"Dirk," Anna sobbed. Tears streamed down her cheeks as the soldier set her in the truck and climbed up after her.

They had been so close to escaping! But now Dirk had to go with Anna. Scowling, he let a soldier grab him and toss him into the rear of the truck, where he landed with a thud next to his sister. The other people in the truck had their hands tied too. Two more guards climbed into the back, and the vehicle roared off.

CHAPTER SEVEN

NAZI RAZZIA TRUCK

"Dirk," Anna sobbed. A soldier glared at them. Dirk couldn't return Anna's hug, so he leaned against her.

"Shh, shh," he said in a soothing tone. But how could he comfort her when this was his fault? He should have taken alleys back to Tante Cora's. But he'd gotten careless, and now the moffen were taking them to who knew where. He shook his head. While they bounced their way down the road in the back of the truck, he looked at the other captives. Most of them wept openly.

"What are we going to do, Dirk?" Tears poured down Anna's cheeks.

"It'll be okay, Anna. I'll think of something." But how could he say that? He had just let her get captured. It was another huge mistake on top of his biggest mistake ever. *I should have done something that night to help Mama. She was sick, and I should have gotten a doctor even though she told me not to.* The truck lurched as the driver shifted, and the captives in the back bumped each other.

They said it wasn't my fault that she died in the middle of the night. But they probably just said that so I wouldn't feel bad. And maybe they wouldn't have said it if they had known the whole story. The part he'd been afraid to tell anyone. He tried to brush his tears away with his shoulder, but with his hands tied behind his back it was impossible. His right hand shook, knocking against his left. He had to pull himself together and figure out a way of escaping from wherever they were going. That would be his only chance of finding Papa and helping Els.

"Where are you taking us?" a prisoner asked a soldier.

"*Halt die Klappe,*" a soldier said, silencing the man and thumping him with the butt of his rifle.

When the guard looked away, a man next to Dirk whispered, "You put up a good fight back there. Is this your sister?" He nodded at Anna.

Too upset to speak, Dirk could only nod.

The man was thin, with close-cropped blond hair and intense blue eyes that darted this way and that, taking in everything. When the guard turned to say something to another soldier, the man next to Dirk spoke again.

"She's lucky she's got you watching out for her."

"Thank you," Dirk managed to say.

After a pause, the man added, "Keep your chin up and look for a way to escape from wherever they're taking us. You will find it."

Dirk sniffed. "Where do you think we're headed?"

"Probably to one of their factories."

Better than going to the Gestapo. Dirk's hand stopped shaking.

Half an hour later, the truck stopped. "*Schnell!*" a soldier ordered, pointing. Other soldiers herded the captives out of the truck and over to a drab, gray warehouse. As they waited next to the building, Dirk stood at the end of a ragged line of workers. As he looked around his new surroundings, a soldier strode toward him with a fifteen-centimeter blade. Dirk tried to step back, but the wall behind him blocked his path. The moment he hit the wall, the soldier grabbed Dirk's shoulder. Dirk gasped and tried to twist away, but the man had a firm grip, and in a lightning motion, he spun Dirk around and cut the rope binding his hands.

"*Dummkopf,*" the soldier said, and then moved to cut the next prisoner's bonds.

Dirk blushed but turned his attention to Anna, resting his hand on her shoulder.

A few minutes later, a sergeant addressed the group of new captives. The man looked to be in his late fifties. He had thick glasses and walked with a pronounced limp, but he held his head high as if he were some man of great importance. Dirk stood next to Anna and near the man who had talked to him in the truck.

"You Dutch aren't our enemies," the sergeant said. "Our war is against the British."

"Then why did you bomb Rotterdam?" the man from the truck said under his breath.

Despite his limp, the sergeant moved from right to left in front of the line of captives, surveying his new slave laborers.

"You're here today," the sergeant continued, "because the English bombed this gun factory. This is where we make weapons for the German army to defend your country from invasion."

"Liar," the man from the truck said out of the corner of his mouth.

"During the attack, workers were killed," the sergeant said as he walked down the line of prisoners. "You will replace them. If you work hard, you will be fed, and no harm will come to you. But if—"

He stopped in front of Anna and stared at her for several seconds, saying nothing. He shifted his gaze to Dirk. "Is this your sister?" he said loud enough for all the workers to hear. Anna clung to Dirk.

"Yes."

The sergeant stepped closer to Anna. He looked down his nose at Dirk. "She's too small and weak to work for the fatherland, and you can't care for her. You're just a young boy."

"I am not a young boy. I'm thirteen years old." Dirk stood tall and pushed out his chest.

The sergeant studied Anna and then smiled. But it wasn't the sort of friendly grin that makes you think things will be better. It was the kind of smile a shark gives his dinner before he eats it in one gulp.

"My friend had a daughter who looked just like you," the sergeant said to Anna. She flinched when he stroked her hair.

"She was about your age and had long blonde hair just like yours. I'll ask him if he wants to adopt you."

"No. She belongs with me." Dirk locked eyes with the sergeant.

Anna threw her arms around Dirk's waist and buried her face in his stomach.

The sergeant took a step closer to Dirk and glared down at him, standing so close Dirk could smell the man's breath. Dirk stood his ground.

The man raised his voice so everyone in line could hear him. "Until I hear back from my friend, your sister may stay, as long as neither of you falls behind in your work or causes trouble."

"She's *my* sister, and you're not taking her." Dirk clenched his fists and glared at the sergeant.

The sergeant glowered at him. "You are speaking to an officer of the Third Reich. Hold your tongue, or I will put you in a prison cell. And then who will watch over your precious sister?" The sergeant turned and limped away, his head still held high.

The man from the truck tapped Dirk on the shoulder. "That sergeant has ears of stone and a heart to match," he whispered.

Dirk nodded.

A guard dismissed the group to walk fifteen meters to the factory. Soldiers directed the men and women to separate rooms to receive their work uniforms. When Dirk released Anna's hand, her pleading eyes spilled over with tears.

He started to speak twice but choked. "Go on," he finally got out. "I'll find you when it's time to eat." He waved her forward, fighting back tears of his own. As she walked away, he patted his pants pocket and felt the outline of the stone. Then he joined the line to receive his new clothing.

While he was in line, Dirk talked to the man from the truck. "Where are we?"

"We're close to Nijmegen. Maybe sixteen kilometers. I recognized a few landmarks on the way here."

Dirk's heart felt a bit lighter. "My grandparents live in Nijmegen." He lowered his voice. "That's where I'll go if I get out of here."

"Not if. *When*," the man from the truck said. "My name's Lars Joosse," he added.

"Nice to meet you, Mr. Joosse. I'm Dirk Ingelse." They shook hands, but a guard approached, so they stopped talking and walked away from each other.

As he stood in line, Dirk looked left and right. He retrieved the stone and orange ribbon from his pocket and slipped them into his mouth. When he got to the front of the line, the guard searched all his pockets and patted him down. With the stone under his tongue and the ribbon in his cheek, Dirk stood statue still. *I hope he doesn't ask me to talk.*

The guard took Dirk's clothes and gave him a uniform— pants and shirt with thin vertical stripes of light and dark gray. The front of the shirt had a red triangle and a five-digit prisoner identification code under it. He walked away and coughed into his hand to get the stone and ribbon out of his mouth. A few moments later, he shoved them into his pocket.

"*Arbeite!*" a soldier shouted and pointed Dirk to a work station. He caught a glimpse of Anna in the distance. She still wore her own pants, but her new shirt hung loosely on her small frame, reaching her knees and looking like a dress that was several sizes too large. *They didn't have her size.* He got a lump in his throat as she walked away with her head down. *Mr. Joosse was right. We will escape.*

By the time Dirk and the other new workers were assigned to their positions, it was nearly one o'clock. A supervisor ordered Dirk to lift ten-kilo boxes of rifle parts and carry them to the head of the assembly line. They got one five-minute break at three o'clock to go to the bathroom.

Dirk's arms and back ached after the first hour, but he said nothing. *I have to find a way out.* He looked around at the layout of the factory and the positioning of the guards. When they wrestled, Papa always said, "Study your opponent. Find a weakness." Dirk clenched his jaw. *I will, Papa.*

CHAPTER EIGHT

AT SIX O'CLOCK, the guards sent the workers to the lunchroom for ten minutes. Dirk looked for Mr. Joosse, but his table was full, so Dirk and Anna took seats near the door. Half of the overhead lights didn't work in the dingy room filled with ramshackle tables and chairs. As Dirk sat with Anna, guards gave each worker two hard biscuits and a small glass of water.

Dirk stared at the food. *It's even less than at Tante Cora's.*

"I want Els and Papa."

"Shh. You have to be quiet," Dirk said. "We're not supposed to talk." He took a bite.

Anna nodded. Then she stood and put her mouth to his ear and whispered, "Ask the Germans where they took Els."

"Sit down, and don't put your mouth to my ear. Turn your head a little toward me when you whisper. I'll hear you, and it won't be so obvious. And we can't ask the Germans where they took Els."

"Why not?"

"We don't want them to know who we are. So *don't* ask them."

"Why?"

Dirk shook his head. "They're the enemy, and now that Els is gone, I'm in charge of you," he said sternly. He held her gaze, hoping she was taking his warning seriously.

A guard walked toward them. Dirk tilted his head slightly in the direction of the guard, hoping Anna picked up on the silent warning so he wouldn't have to shush her with the guard so close. By the time the man walked past them, they had both finished their meager rations.

Anna picked up the few biscuit crumbs remaining from her meal and popped them in her mouth. She stared at the spot on the table where the crumbs had been. "I'm still hungry, Dirk," she said.

"I know, I know." He looked for the guard and then quickly patted her on the back. "I'm hungry too. But I'll get us out of here," he whispered out of the side of his mouth. "We have to be strong. Can you do that until I figure out a way to escape?"

"I guess." A tear slid down her cheek. She turned her hands palms up, revealing large blisters. "It hurts," she whimpered.

Dirk grimaced. "Yes, it hurts, Anna." *I hate the Nazis.* He pounded his fists into his thighs.

"Your hands will get tough, and then they won't hurt so much." He turned his head away so she wouldn't see the tears in his eyes.

A loud bell rang. Workers trudged back to their stations.

"Don't forget," a quiet male voice behind Dirk said.

Dirk snapped his head around to see Mr. Joosse.

"Don't forget. You will escape." He left for his work station.

When the dismissal bell rang at nine o'clock, exhausted laborers shuffled to a nearby empty warehouse.

The low-ceiling cinder block structure was three times the size of the Ingelses' barn on the farm. Each worker received one small blanket, just big enough to cover two-thirds of Dirk's body. All around them, the workers, weak with fatigue, staggered into the warehouse and collapsed into sleep. Dirk was as tired as any of them, but before surrendering to sleep, he scanned the building with wary eyes. He noted the only door to the building, guarded by two soldiers, and the small windows four meters above the floor.

He put his arm around Anna's shoulder. "I'm going to get us out of here."

"You should ask God to help us," she told him. "That's what Mama and Papa would do."

It's hard to believe in that with everything that's happened. He fidgeted with a button on his shirt. "I have something to show you," he said. He reached in his pants pocket and pulled out the orange ribbon.

Anna's tired face brightened. "My ribbon from Papa!" she said, reaching for it. "The one he sent us to let us know that he still—"

"Shh. Not so loud." But it felt good to see her happy. "I have the stone he sent me too." He tapped his pocket.

"Can I sleep with the ribbon?"

"Sure. But cover it with your hands so the guards won't see it."

"Why?"

"Papa sent you an orange ribbon because the Dutch royal family is the House of Orange," Dirk said.

"Uh-huh."

"The orange ribbon shows you're loyal to the Netherlands, not Germany." He paused. "The soldiers will be really mad if they see it."

"Okay," she said. "But I'm still hungry." She'd grown thinner since leaving the farm. Everything was thinner—her arms and legs. Even her face was thinner.

Compassion washed over Dirk like a big wave from the North Atlantic. Anna looked up at him with her big blue eyes. If only he had something to give her to eat. Anything at all.

He adjusted her blanket. "Close your eyes, Anna, and I'll tell you a story about Princess Anna and the petticoats."

"Make her play hide-and-go-seek, and nobody knows where she hides."

"All right," Dirk said.

Anna held Papa's ribbon tightly against her cheek and closed her eyes. By the time Dirk was one minute into the story, she'd fallen asleep. He scanned the room and noted that the guards were still by the door. He kept his eyes on them as he reached into his pocket, pulled out the stone, and rubbed it between his thumb and index finger. *This stone and Anna are all I have left from Mama and Papa.*

For the next few days, the long hours of work dragged on for Dirk. One day he and Mr. Joosse carried boxes to the other end of the factory. In a low tone Mr. Joosse said, "We'll find a way out of here."

"How?" Dirk asked.

"I don't know. But I've been in worse situations. When the Germans bombed Rotterdam, there were flames everywhere. I escaped being burned alive by jumping into the river. After the bombing, the city burned for three days." He looked Dirk in the eye. "We *will* escape. Keep telling yourself that."

"I will, but I'm worried about my sister. Every day she's a little thinner, and I'm getting weaker too," Dirk said.

"I know," Mr. Joosse said. "But we will get out of here."

Though Dirk and Anna worked in different areas, they ate together, and they slept next to each other every night. Five days after they were brought to the gun factory, the sergeant limped up to Dirk when the workers were lined up for morning roll call. "I have wonderful news," he said, flashing his hungry shark smile again. "My friend has decided to adopt your sister. First thing tomorrow morning I will put her on a train to Germany. She'll have a family again."

Dirk scowled. "She has a family now. *I'm* her family!"

Mr. Joosse was standing next to Dirk. He glared at the sergeant. "There will be a war crimes trial after Germany loses the war," he said.

The sergeant smirked. "But we are winning the war."

"If you're winning, why are the only planes we see overhead Allied bombers and fighters on their way to crush your war factories?"

"I don't have to listen to you."

"Apparently you don't have to listen to your conscience either, since you're sending a little girl away from the only family she has left."

"Is this true?" the sergeant said to Dirk.

He nodded.

"Well then, it is for her good that she will go to a bigger family. A better one."

Raising his voice, Mr. Joosse said, "Only a weak man would try to show his strength by picking on a little girl."

The sergeant shook his head. "Your words don't threaten me at all, but I find you dull. Guard! Take this man to solitary confinement as punishment for boring me."

As the guard led Mr. Joosse away, the sergeant turned to Dirk. "I could lock you up too, but I won't. Instead I will allow you to have the privilege of telling your sister the good news."

Dirk held the sergeant's cold gaze. "You can't take her! She's my sister."

The man poked Dirk's chest with his index finger. "A young boy is in no position to tell an officer of the Wehrmacht what he cannot do." He turned and walked away.

Dirk had to figure out a way to escape right away, and now he couldn't even ask Mr. Joosse for advice. What could he do? Despite what Mr. Joosse had kept saying, it seemed to Dirk like there was no way to get out.

A memory flashed. He and Papa had been in the barn. After they'd finished chores, they'd wrestled for a few minutes. The last thing Papa said to him that time was about avoiding getting pinned in wrestling. He'd looked Dirk in the eye and put his hands on Dirk's shoulders as he said, "Never give up. Your opponent may get overconfident or careless. Keep trying."

I will, Papa.

That night, when he met Anna in the warehouse, Dirk

steered her to a wall. She stumbled with fatigue as she walked, so he scooped her up in his arms. He winced as he put his arms around her skinny body. *They're starving her!* It was one more reason they had to find a way out.

"Let's sleep here," he said. He looked around the large room, then leaned close to Anna and whispered, "We have to escape tonight. You sleep. In a little while, I'll wake you up, and we'll get out of here."

"Promise?"

"Yes."

"I want Oma and Opa," Anna said as she lay down on the floor.

"I know," he said. He tucked her blanket around her shoulders. "I'll get us out of here and figure out a way to go to their house. It's not that far."

"Can I have my ribbon?"

"Sure." He fished it out of his pocket but held it out of her reach. "Promise me you'll run when I tell you to?"

"Uh-huh," she said. She clasped the ribbon with both hands and pulled it to her face. "I'm hungry, Dirk."

How many times had she said that to him? But he had no good response to give her.

"Uh . . . Pull your legs up and scrunch them against your stomach, like I'm doing, so your belly won't feel so empty." He lifted his legs to his midsection and held them there with his arms.

"Will that help?"

"Oh, sure," he said, avoiding eye contact, "but it may take five or ten minutes before you feel the difference."

He put her head in his lap, spread her blanket over her, and started the Princess Anna story. "You don't tell it as good as Tante Cora," she said.

"You miss her, don't you?"

"Uh-huh. Give Princess Anna a pony," she said. "A talking pony, and the pony only talks to the princess."

"Once upon a time there was a princess named Anna." She closed her eyes. "One day the king gave her a beautiful pony, for her birthday."

"Don't forget, it's a talking pony," she said with a big yawn.

"And as soon as the princess and the pony were alone, it talked to her."

Anna smiled. Soon her smile faded and her breathing slowed.

"And that night Anna and her brother rode the pony away from the Germans," Dirk added in a whisper.

Two guards stood by the warehouse exit. If he waited, maybe they would get sleepy. Leaning against the wall, he dozed off several times. He pinched himself and shook his head. In the dark, it was hard to tell, but a guard seemed to stare at him.

They would be suspicious of anyone who was awake. The best way to fool them was to look asleep. Not only that, but Dirk and Anna could be walking all night, and a little rest now would do them good. Dirk relaxed and let his chin drop to his chest. He could open his eyes, but what if the guard was watching? He might as well give the guards a chance to get sleepy. Just a few more minutes.

CHAPTER NINE

A PIERCING ALARM shattered the silence as morning rays entered the warehouse windows. Dirk winced at the noise, rubbed his eyes, and stretched his arms and legs to get rid of the stiffness from sleeping on the hard floor.

Then with a jolt, he sat up. *No! I fell asleep!*

The sound he was hearing was an air-raid siren! The factory was under attack! If they somehow survived, the Germans would send Anna away.

"Dirk!" Anna wailed. He pulled her close, snatched her orange ribbon off the ground, and stuffed it into his pocket. Workers huddled in corners of the building, trying to shield themselves from the coming attack. But that wouldn't help if the whole building got destroyed. There was no sign of the guards. Dirk shuddered and stood.

An explosion outside their building shook the ground, and he almost lost his balance. Anna clung to him, her nails digging into his skin.

Boom! "Agh!" they cried out and clutched their ears. Jagged beams and shingles fell from the roof on the other side of the building and landed on the floor with a loud *whump*.

"What do we do?" Anna cried.

"We're getting out of here. Run!"

"Are you sure?"

"Yes. The guards have taken cover. Go!"

"But what about the bombs?"

"There's no bomb shelter for us workers. They don't care what happens to us. If we die in the attack, they'll just grab more workers."

Some of Papa's words sliced through the chaos: *"Sometimes you have to take a chance, because it's the only chance you have."* He had said that more times than Dirk could remember.

"Come on!" He grabbed Anna's hand. Moments later, they were outside the building. Another bomb exploded, and they stumbled.

Dirk and Anna flinched at the sudden blast of a truck exploding. Red and orange flames from the vehicle shot three meters high.

A bomb had blasted a big hole in the fence, and Dirk veered toward the opening. But after they ran through the gap, he skidded to a stop. He stared at the sign between them and the road—*Achtung! Minenfeld.*

"Why did you stop?" Anna asked.

"We'll get blown up if we walk through that minefield." He looked left and right. "But there has to be a way of getting through." He had to find a way out quickly, or they would be recaptured after the attack ended. *Why isn't God helping us?*

He bent over and stared at the ground in front of him. A series of footprints zigzagged through the dirt all the way to the other side of the minefield.

"That's it," he said.

"What?" Lines of fear creased Anna's forehead.

"There's a path through the minefield. See?" He pointed. "Let's go!"

Her lower lip quivered. "I'm scared! What if I step in the wrong spot?"

"Follow me," he said. He took her hand and carefully placed his feet in the footprints. "Step where I step, Anna."

A few moments later, he stopped suddenly. Anna bumped him from behind and nearly knocked him over. "Be careful!" he said.

Dirk kneeled and squinted at the ground. *Where is the path?* He could see the footprints a couple of meters ahead, but just in front of him they had been smudged so they were unrecognizable.

Another blast echoed behind them. *We've got to keep going.* Dirk lifted his foot to continue.

Just then the sun burst through an opening in the clouds. The sudden brightness revealed a portion of metal that poked out of the dirt less than a meter in front of Dirk. *That could only be one thing.* He swallowed hard as he stared at the place where he had almost put his foot.

"This way," he said and headed toward the place where the footprints clearly showed. He released Anna's hand and motioned her to stay a little farther behind him, just in case. But they both had to make it through. What if something happened to him—how would Anna escape on her own? Dirk advanced slowly, placing one foot barely in front of the other, hardly daring to breathe. Finally he reached the place where he could see clear footprints. He resumed his pace and turned each time the prints did, all the way to the road.

"We made it!" he exclaimed. "Come over this way." He motioned toward the weeds and bushes along the side of the road. "They'll see us if we keep walking on the road. We have to run."

They started jogging along the side of the road. "Slow down," Anna soon begged.

"You have to run, Anna. They'll come looking for us any minute." It had been a few minutes now since they'd heard a bomb explode.

Anna's breath surged in ragged gasps, and soon they both slowed to a fast walk.

If they see us, we're both too weak to outrun them. "We need to find a farm," Dirk said.

"Why?" Anna asked.

"Farms have places to hide, and they have food," Dirk said.

"Oh."

In the distance several people riding bikes headed toward Dirk and Anna. He motioned for Anna to hide behind a bush. He wanted to ask them for directions to a farm, but no one would risk arrest by helping two people in prison uniforms this close to a work camp.

It was a race against time. If they didn't find a farm quickly, they would be overtaken by a search party. Would they shoot even kids for escaping?

A few minutes later, Dirk spotted a military vehicle driving in their direction. He pulled Anna behind some heavy bushes and lowered her to the ground. She gasped when the German truck roared past. A minute later he helped her to her feet.

"I'm cold, and I'm hungry," she whimpered.

"I know it's hard without a coat," Dirk said, "but the sun is out, and it'll warm us a little. We'll find a farm soon and ask for food." He watched for more vehicles. It was his fault they'd gotten caught in the razzia near Tante Cora's. He wouldn't let anything like that happen again. They resumed walking.

Thirty minutes later, Anna said, "Look! Up there." She pointed ahead. When Dirk followed her gaze and saw a small barn surrounded by fields, he smiled.

"We have to get there without anyone seeing us," he said. He stared at the barn. A farm promised shelter, safety, and food—everything they hadn't had since Tante Cora's.

The low rumble of approaching vehicles grew louder, and Dirk glanced over his shoulder. *Germans!* He grabbed Anna and dove for cover into the tall weeds behind a large tree. Two trucks skidded to a stop on the road fewer than ten meters away. *Why did the soldiers have to come now when we're so close to safety?*

Dirk and Anna lay motionless on the ground. If he had seen the trucks as they approached, the soldiers might just as easily have seen them, but maybe they were just guessing that escaped workers would hide in the tall weeds. Dirk's heart thumped, and his palms got sweaty. *Is this what the Jews feel like when the Nazis hunt them?* His throat tightened.

"What's happening?" Anna asked. Dirk glared at her and held his finger to his lips in a silent "Shh!"

"*Schnell! Schnell!*" a gruff voice barked. They heard soldiers jump from the trucks and hurry toward them.

It's the sergeant from the gun factory. Dirk froze. He heard the scrunch, scrunch of boots on gravel and then a quiet swish of trousers brushing weeds. He shuddered as the steps came closer and closer. Anna clung to Dirk.

Dirk detected a distant drone that quickly grew louder. *Another truck? No!* He strained to hear. *A plane!*

"*Achtung! Fallt zu Boden!*" the sergeant shouted. Following the order, the soldiers lunged to the ground, grunting as they landed. Dirk pulled Anna closer to him and kept his head down as the plane approached from the other side of the large tree near them. *It's diving!* The fighter's guns chattered. Bullets raked the weeds, ripped bark off the tree, and stirred up dust. Amid the roar of the attack, several soldiers cried out. Dirk put his hand over Anna's eyes to shield her from the light debris that showered them.

The plane zoomed overhead. *Probably a British Spitfire or an American P-51.* Without raising his head, Dirk chanced a quick look up as the plane banked in a tight turn. Papa had taught him to identify planes, and this one stood out against the blue sky with its black-and-white checkerboard nose and the big white star on the side. *P-51 Mustang.* Dirk buried his face in the weeds. *Come back. You have to come back.*

The Germans scrambled to their feet and shot at the retreating plane. Dirk watched as it flew away. *Come back!*

The sergeant barked orders, and the soldiers resumed

their search pattern. *No!* Dirk held his breath as a soldier drew nearer. He and Anna clutched each other more tightly.

Then a familiar noise returned. The plane approached from a different direction, so Dirk and Anna scrambled to remain shielded by the tree. The P-51 dropped low, and all six guns blazed at the enemy who huddled on the ground. Something exploded, and the plane roared overhead and flew away.

The sergeant shouted orders, but they were hard to make out over the noise of other soldiers' talking and groaning. A truck roared to life, boots scuffled on the pavement, and then the truck drove away. After a minute of silence, Dirk raised his head and stared at the flames which devoured the second German truck on the road.

"You can sit up," he told Anna.

He scanned the road left and right. It would feel good to stand near the fire and get warm for once. But they would be in plain view on the road, and they couldn't risk being near the truck if it blew up.

"We have to get in that barn before another vehicle comes by," Dirk said. "The crops were harvested a long time ago, and that means anyone will be able to see us from the road." They walked to a wood fence which marked the farm's border.

After they crawled through the fence, Dirk stood, checked the road again for vehicles, and took a deep breath. Everything was on the line now. He had to pick the right time to run, or they would be caught by a passing patrol.

"Ready to run as fast as you can?"

"Yes."

"Go!" He nudged Anna and jogged behind her.

Halfway to the barn, she fell and clutched her ankle. "Ow! I twisted it."

Not now! He shot a panicked look toward the street. *Nothing there.* Dirk crouched in front of Anna with his back turned toward her. "Climb on and hold on tight!" If an enemy vehicle appeared while they ran across the field, he would drop to the ground and hope that at this distance, the soldiers wouldn't notice.

Dirk sprinted toward the barn. He shot a look over his shoulder, then ran as fast as he could without stumbling, keeping an ear toward the road. He faltered a few times where the ground was bumpy but kept his balance. Carrying Anna on his back, he tired quickly. His lungs burned, and his legs ached, but he forced himself to keep up his pace. *Keep going. Almost there.*

When they reached the barn, Dirk set Anna on a bale of hay. He dropped next to her, chest heaving. A few chickens pecked for food on the other side of the barn, but the stalls were empty. *Thanks to the Germans.*

"Hide behind the hay bales while I get us a drink," Dirk said. He glanced back to be sure she was out of sight, then grabbed a metal cup from a shelf near the barn door. He looked both ways and dipped the cup in a rain barrel. After he drank the first cupful, he refilled it.

"Here you go," he said, bringing the cup back to Anna. She gulped it down. Then she frowned.

"What's wrong? Still thirsty?"

"No," she said. "I have to pee."

CHAPTER TEN

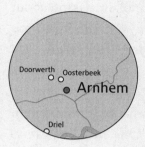

GESTAPO INTERROGATION CENTER
OOSTERBEEK
NOVEMBER 22

How LONG had she been in prison? Ten days? Els wasn't sure. As November trudged toward December, her cell grew steadily colder. But she would not break under pressure. Each night she clutched her pebble to her chest. "Heart of stone," she whispered before falling asleep. She whispered it again when she woke up, and when she returned the pebble to its hiding place in the corner before going for questioning. They'd never get secrets from her.

But while Els's spirit remained strong, her stamina declined. Her undernourished body shivered, burning energy she didn't have to spare. She couldn't believe how thin her arms and legs had become and how much effort walking now required. Though she remained resolute in her determination to keep secrets from the Germans, now it was a quiet determination because she no longer had the energy she'd had when she was first captured.

First thing in the morning, after a few scraps of bread and a bowl of watery soup, the daily assault on her ears and emotions began. Most days it was questions of every kind about Papa. They demanded to know where he was, who his friends were, where he hid the Jews, and how he helped Allied pilots to escape. Always Els responded to the questions with evasive replies or silence.

One day the tactic was eight straight hours of insults, with a fresh interrogator every two hours. One criticized everything that was Dutch. "The Dutch army didn't even last one week against the might of the German army, because the Dutch people are weak," he began. "The Dutch winter is too rainy, and the Netherlands' art and literature are pathetic compared to the greatness of German culture." He went on to ridicule Dutch licorice, dikes, canals, and windmills.

But the first man seemed to be just a warm-up act for the next one, who targeted her family. "Your father left home because your mother was extremely ugly. He hates you and your siblings for being nothing but brats. Your little sister, Anna, is stupid, and your brother, Dirk, is now collaborating with the Germans." They would say anything to get Els to say something, even if it was an angry outburst in response to some insult splashed in her face. But she told them nothing.

The next day no one came to unleash angry questions or abrasive insults. They were setting her up for something. But what? Everything they did was geared to force her to talk.

Everything. So this was part of that plan. But what would they do?

Els guessed that since the Nazis couldn't wear her down with words, they had changed tactics to isolation. She relished the relief from their constant verbal bombardment. She rested near her cell door, and every time she heard footsteps, she moaned about how terrible it was to be alone and not see another human being. As soon as the passerby was out of earshot, she resumed dozing. Then she started saying the same things when no one was near, in case they had tiptoed to her door to be sure it wasn't just an act.

But what if during her solitude they were planning something more awful than she could imagine? She bit her lip.

The next day she was alone all day until after she had eaten the bits of food which the Germans called her dinner. A hulking guard yanked open the door to Els's cell and pushed a woman inside. "We have had many arrests, and all the cells must now hold two prisoners," he told Els. He shoved the newcomer to the center of the room, and it seemed that the cell door clanged shut even before the disheveled woman crumpled in a heap on the floor.

Els had been dozing, but she sat up with a jerk and studied the new arrival. The woman didn't move. The only sound that came from her was a faint moaning, as if she didn't have the strength to produce anything louder. The woman's face was crumpled in pain, and her breathing was labored. *Poor thing.* What terrible things had the Nazi goons inflicted on her?

Els moved to her side and slid her mattress—the only one

in the cell—next to the newcomer. "Do you want to lie on this? Can you roll over?" she whispered.

"Ohh," the woman said after a pause. She rolled over onto the thin mattress but winced and clutched her left leg below the knee.

"I wish I could do something to help you feel better," Els said, looking into the woman's eyes.

"Thank you," the woman managed to get out.

Els watched the other woman in silence for a while. It would be good to have someone to talk to who wasn't accusing her or slapping her in the face.

"What did the moffen do to you?" Els asked gently as she reached out and lightly touched the woman on the shoulder.

"Everything," the woman said through clenched teeth. She groaned. "We hid Jews in our attic, but their baby cried while a neighbor visited. Two hours later the Gestapo came. So the moffen did this," she said, pointing weakly to her lower leg. "I think it's broken."

Els shook her head. "Ohhh. That's terrible."

The woman took several deep breaths. "What's your name?"

"Elisabeth," Els replied without hesitation. It was the standard name she gave to people she didn't know well. It was her mother's name, and with the way the Nazis were after information about Papa, the fewer people who knew Els's real name, the better. Besides, it felt good to say her mother's name again.

"I'm Roos," the other woman said with a great deal of effort. Els nodded.

"How long have you been in here?" Roos asked Els.

"About ten days, I think."

"What's it like in here?" she asked, her head still on the mattress and her eyes closed.

"Every morning starts with stale dark bread, mostly made of sawdust." Els snorted. "Those few pieces of food are followed by hours of harsh interrogation. What they call supper is bread and so-called soup—water with a few potato peels and some rotten cabbage. And then it's time to sleep on this skinny mattress." She shook her head. "The next day it starts all over again." She leaned closer to Roos and whispered, "What's happening with the war?"

Roos grimaced, looked at the small window in the cell door, and said, "The Americans are moving across France."

"Oh, that's good." Els smiled. "Any other news?"

"The British sank the German battleship *Tirpitz*." Roos was quiet for a while, then asked, "Where are you from?"

"Duindorp." It was another answer she often gave to people to protect her true identity. "Do you know where that is?"

"Yes. It's near Scheveningen."

"That's right," Els said with a slight smile. After a brief silence, she asked, "Where are you from?"

The woman was slow to reply, as if even talking took energy out of her. "Arnhem," she finally said.

"I'm sorry for bothering you. If you'd rather rest and not talk, I understand," Els said. "It's just so good to have someone to talk to."

"I like . . . talking too," Roos said. After a pause she winced and added, "It takes my mind off the pain."

"The last time I visited Arnhem we saw the Doorwerth Castle," Els said.

The woman nodded slightly.

"It's hard to believe it hasn't been damaged by the war," Els added.

"There is a lot of Dutch history in that building," Roos said.

Els nodded. "Before the war, my papa delivered food from farms to families in the area. He made a lot of deliveries to the castle."

Roos's eyes opened. "Your papa must have met a lot of people with a job like that."

"Yes, he did. He has a way of making customers feel like friends."

With effort, Roos scooched to the nearest wall, grunted, and partially sat up, leaning on the wall for support. She looked at Els. "Where is your papa now? I hope he's all right."

"I hope so too," Els said. "But you are not from Arnhem. Doorwerth Castle was badly damaged two months ago, and everyone in Arnhem knows it. The Nazis put you in this cell to get me to let something slip about Papa. A lot of other things gave you away, but I won't tell you what you did wrong, because I don't teach traitors how to fix their stories. You want to know about my papa? I'll tell you this. He taught me to read people like a book," Els said, glaring at the other woman, "and yours has an unhappy ending."

"That isn't true. I'm not a collaborator," Roos said with a furrowed forehead.

"It *is* true. I am done talking to you about anything."

"You have to believe me," Roos said with pleading eyes. Els said nothing. She just folded her arms and glared at the other woman.

The two women were quiet. Five minutes later the cell door opened, and a guard motioned for Roos to follow him. She clambered to her feet and walked out, showing no sign of her former leg pain.

Els stared at the cell door. The Nazis would stop at nothing to get information about Papa. Cruelty had failed, so they'd resorted to treachery. She smiled. That meant Papa was a real thorn in their side. And they still had no idea where he was.

Roos, or whatever her name really was, thought she might fool Els. But that woman was too well fed to be in the Resistance, she showed too much interest at the first mention of Papa, and she'd mispronounced Scheveningen, the way Germans do.

Els jerked the mattress from where the impostor had lain on it and shoved it back to its previous position. She brushed the surface with her hand; she wanted no trace of the betrayer left on it. The moffen had tried and failed again to get her to talk.

She picked up the pebble in the corner and mouthed, "Heart of stone."

CHAPTER ELEVEN

FARMHOUSE NEAR DRIEL

DIRK STUDIED THE HOUSE for several minutes, but no one entered or left. "I'm going to knock on the door now, Anna."

"Wait!" Anna said. "What if they give us back to the Germans?"

Dirk glanced at the work uniforms they still wore, and a chill shot up his spine. "There are a lot of good Dutch people, Anna, and most of the people who were helping the Germans are scared to do that now because the Germans are losing."

"But what if they take us back to the gun factory?"

Dirk's right hand twitched, and he thrust it into his pocket.

"Well," he gulped, "then we'll just have to escape again. But sometimes you have to take a chance, because it's the only chance you have." He kneeled in front of her and looked her in the eye. "If they promise to help, then I'll come get you."

"And they'll take us to Oma and Opa's house?" Anna squealed.

"I hope so," Dirk said. "How is your ankle?"

"It's okay."

"Good." He walked to the barn door and stared across the field. He motioned to Anna. "Come over here. Do you see that next house?"

"Uh-huh."

"Here's what you need to do." His voice cracked. "If I don't come back to the barn . . ." He turned away and took several deep breaths. He turned back to her and said, his voice still shaky, "If I, uh, stay in the house, I want you to hide in this barn until dark and then walk to that next farm." He pointed with his left hand. "Ask them to help you get to Oma and Opa's. Understand?"

"Uh-huh. But how will you get to Oma and Opa's?" She squinted at him, studying his expression.

"I'll . . . uh . . . have to find a different way to their house." He looked away. *Or maybe I'll never see you again.*

He led Anna to a stall. "You need to hide here until I come back for you."

She hugged him hard.

"It will be all right," he said, trying to convince both himself and Anna before he walked toward the back door of the farmhouse. When he looked back at the barn, Anna was standing in the doorway of the stall, so he motioned for her to move out of sight. He slowly climbed the porch steps. What would the farmer say? What if something went wrong? He knocked and waited, heart pounding.

The door swung open, and Dirk looked into the face of an elderly Dutch farmer. His face and hands were weathered by the sun, and his hair was silver.

"Who are you?" the man asked, grim faced.

"My name's Dirk. We, I mean, I escaped from the Germans." He pointed at his uniform. "Will you help me get to my oma and opa's house?"

The farmer waved his hands and mouthed a few words. "What?"

"I'm sorry. I can't help you," the farmer whispered and started to close the door.

"Tell him to come in," a deep male voice inside the house ordered. The farmer hesitated. "Tell him to come in," the voice demanded. The farmer weakly motioned for Dirk to enter. Dirk stepped into the kitchen, and his eyes grew wide. A tall uniformed German officer stood next to the kitchen sink. Dirk edged toward the door.

"Don't move," the officer ordered.

Dirk froze.

"Who's the boy?" the officer asked.

"I don't know," the farmer said.

"I will deal with him later. But I believe that you are helping the Resistance."

"That isn't true," the farmer said.

The officer glared at him, then nodded at Dirk. "Then why did an escapee come here? Someone sent him."

"I don't work for the Resistance," the farmer said.

Oh no! Anna was right. Dirk shifted his eyes back and forth between the two men.

A woman who appeared to be a few years younger than the farmer entered the room and rushed to the farmer's side. She was short and plump, with short brown hair.

"Prove you do not help the Resistance," the officer said as he rested his right hand on the Luger in its holster.

Dirk's eyes darted around the room. He was too far away from the door to escape. The same thing for both windows.

"It's all I can do to survive with what little we have left," the man answered. "I can't help the Resistance or anyone else."

Does that include Anna and me?

"Prove it!" the German demanded.

"I can't. I can't prove something I haven't done." The farmer's nostrils flared. "You might as well ask me to show you the horses and cows your army stole from me," he said. "And you might as well ask me for crops, even though my fields were stripped bare to feed your soldiers."

Don't make him mad! Dirk shifted his stance. For a moment the officer glared at him and then turned his attention back to the farmer's wife. He stared at her for a few moments, stone faced.

What's he going to do? Dirk's palms were sweaty.

As the officer pulled the pistol from its holster, Dirk's breathing became shallow. His eyes darted around the room. There was no furniture close enough to dive behind if the Nazi started shooting. What should he do? *Papa would know.* Seconds dragged by.

The officer returned the gun to its holster. "I had to threaten you like that to know for sure if you were collaborators," the officer said. "If you were, you would have told me when I accused you of working with the Resistance." He shook his head. "I could not risk you reporting me to the German army."

Dirk studied him. What kind of man would pull a gun on an innocent farmer and his wife just to be sure of his own safety?

The farmer put his arm around his wife, who stared with wide eyes at the officer.

"As you know, the American army is in Nijmegen. When they renew their offensive, I will surrender to them," the officer said. "Until then, I will stay in your home. You will give me food and shelter. Understand?"

The farmer's wife shot a frightened look at her husband. He wiped perspiration from his forehead with his handkerchief. He nodded.

"What about me?" Dirk asked the farmer. "You said you couldn't help anyone. W-w-will you help me get to my grandparents' house?"

The farmer looked at the officer but didn't respond.

"Please?" Dirk added.

"Where do they live?" the farmer asked.

"In Nijmegen," Dirk said.

"That's not very far away. When the Americans come, we'll ask them to take you there."

No more running and no more hiding! *We're safe!* And now they had a chance at finding Papa and rescuing Els. "My sister's in the barn. I waited to tell you until I knew you would help us."

The German nodded. "It's hard to know who you can trust in wartime."

CHAPTER TWELVE

DIRK RAN to the barn. "Anna, it's safe to come to the house."

His sister peeked out of the stall where he'd told her to hide. Tears poured down her face.

"Why are you crying?" he asked.

"You were gone so long. I thought something bad happened to you." She buried her face in his chest.

"No, I'm fine."

"I was so scared," she said.

He bent down and looked her in the eye. "Don't be afraid," he said, hugging her. "There's a German officer, but he said he left the army. We're going to be all right." Telling her about how the man had threatened the farmer's wife would do her no good. Once again it would be up to Dirk to protect Anna because he knew more about the possible danger.

Anna dried her tears on her sleeve, and they walked to the house.

"You're still wearing your uniforms from the gun factory,"

the farmer said. "If anyone sees you, there'll be big trouble for you and us. We don't have the right size clothes for you or your sister. We'll have to see what we can come up with."

That evening the farmer, his wife, Dirk, Anna, and the German officer shared a meal. The farmer and his wife were Mr. and Mrs. ten Haken, and the German officer was Colonel Fleischer. The hot food tasted good—not like the dry, stale biscuits the Nazis had fed them at the work camp. Dirk should have thoroughly enjoyed having enough to eat, but something bothered him about Colonel Fleischer, and he couldn't put his finger on it.

That night, Dirk and Anna climbed the stairs to a bedroom on the third floor. "A real bed with sheets," she said. "And we're going to see Oma and Opa, right?"

"I think so. I mean, yes. That's what Mr. ten Haken said."

"I want you to pray with me, Dirk. Like Els always did."

But Dirk's mind was on other things. What awful things had the Nazis done to Els by now? Could Dirk find Papa in time to rescue her?

"Come on, Dirk. Papa and Els always said to keep your hopes up and your prayers strong. You have to."

He hesitated. It was hard to pray after all that had happened. But Anna had been through a horrible experience at the gun factory, was still separated from her sister and father, and now she was asking him for just a small favor.

"Pray for Papa and for Els to be safe and pray that—"

"Okay, okay." He smiled. "I get the idea." He cleared his throat and bowed his head. "Keep us safe, and protect Papa and Els. And help us find Papa. Amen."

"You forgot Tante Cora."

"And help Tante Cora, too. Amen," he said.

Anna put her arms around his neck and squeezed tight. Dirk returned the hug and handed her the orange ribbon. "I want a story," she said in a drowsy mumble.

"All right. Once upon a time there was a princess named Anna," he whispered slowly. "She had a beautiful petticoat that was her favorite."

"Make it orange this time," she said.

"She had many petticoats, but she loved her orange one best of all."

Anna's hand relaxed, and the ribbon slipped out of her grasp.

Dirk lowered his voice. "One day she went for a walk in the forest, and when she found a dark path—" He looked at his sleeping sister. "She wasn't afraid," he continued, "because she knew her big brother would do anything to protect her. *Anything.*"

He stood slowly and pulled a blanket up to her chin. "I kept my promise, Mama. I kept Anna safe."

Shortly after midnight, Dirk dreamed that a figure stood in the doorway of the bedroom where he and Anna slept. Moonlight leaked around the edges of the window shade, dimly lighting the visitor. At first there was no sound, but when the figure stepped into the room, the floor creaked. A coat with a large hood concealed the visitor's face until she threw back the hood, revealing a gentle smile.

Mama! Dirk tried to reach his hand toward her, but he couldn't move.

It couldn't be her. As much as he longed for it to be her, it couldn't be.

But it *was* her. He tried to speak, but his voice was as useless as his limbs. Mama held a finger to her lips and smiled.

"Don't tell them who you are, Dirk."

He furrowed his brow. *Don't tell who?* He listened intently.

"Don't tell them who you are or who Papa is."

He tried to ask her why, but he still couldn't speak.

"I have to go, but promise me you won't let them find out. I love you, Dirk." She turned away and vanished. Then he woke.

"Mama!" he finally called out. She had looked so real and alive.

"Who was she warning me about?" he whispered. He sat up. Papa had told him stories of people in the Bible who were warned by dreams. Dirk rubbed his chin. Was this dream a warning? Why did he have to figure this out by himself? If only he could ask Papa.

The dream couldn't be a warning about the farmer. He was helping them. Dirk fiddled with the edge of the blanket. It had to be the German officer. "He'll try to make us talk," he said under his breath. He got out of bed and walked back and forth. "That's why Mama warned me." He turned toward the closed bedroom door and imagined addressing the man who claimed he was no longer the enemy. "You're not getting anything out of me or Anna," he hissed. He pushed his hand in his pocket and felt the stone from Papa. His fingers lingered over its smooth surfaces. "I won't tell him anything about you, Papa."

Papa and Els always said, "Keep your hopes up and your prayers strong." I miss you, Papa.

Dirk thought back to a conversation he'd overheard months earlier. He had woken up hungry in the middle of the night and walked downstairs to get something to eat. But he had stopped halfway down when he heard voices in the kitchen. Mama was still alive then, and he recognized her voice, but not the other two. He edged down another step or two and cupped his hands behind his ears.

He caught only parts of sentences. "That's going to be dangerous for the Dutch Resistance Movement . . . help the underdivers and the Jews . . . Allied pilots shot down," a man's voice said. " . . . get back to England . . . very dangerous . . . Gestapo raids," replied a woman's voice.

Dirk tried to recognize the voices. One was Mama's, and another sounded like their neighbor Mr. van Nort, but he couldn't be sure.

The third person said something that Dirk couldn't make out. He peeked around the corner of the stairway and saw three figures huddled around a small light in the center of the kitchen table. That little candle would compromise their night vision, so they wouldn't see him in the darkness on the steps. Papa had taught him that.

Mama was at the kitchen table, and so was Mr. van Nort, but who was the other person? And what were underdivers? Over the next several minutes, Dirk overheard just a few more phrases. Then the kitchen went dark, the front door creaked, and footsteps came toward him. He closed his eyes and pretended to be asleep, leaning against the wall.

"I know you're awake," Mama said as she sat on the stairs next to him. "How long did you listen to our conversation?"

"I was hungry, Mama, and I came down to get something to eat."

"How much did you hear?" She put her face in front of his, holding his gaze.

"I . . . I couldn't help it. I heard a little, and I was curious."

"What did you hear?"

"What's an underdiver?" He watched her closely.

She pressed her lips together. "The underdivers are the Jews and other people who hide from the Nazis."

"Oh."

"The less you know, the safer you'll be. And don't tell anyone what you heard, or what you think you heard."

"I won't, Mama. Do Anna and Els know?"

"Anna doesn't, and don't tell her. Els knows some things." Mama waved her index finger at him. "But don't discuss this with her either."

"I won't, but who were you talking to in the kitchen? Mr. van Nort and who else? You're all in the Resistance, aren't you?"

She hesitated and put her hand on his shoulder.

"If anything happens to me," she said, "Els will be in charge of you and Anna. And if anything happens to Els, you'll be in charge of Anna. Then you should take Anna to Tante Cora's. Understand?"

"Yes," Dirk said.

Mama hugged him tightly.

"What do you mean? What could happen to you?"

"You came down here because you were hungry. Eat something and go back to bed."

She waited as he spread two slices of bread with butter and ate them. As he settled back into bed, he stared at the ceiling in the dark. Papa *was* a Resistance fighter. Why else would Mama forbid Dirk to tell anyone what he had heard?

Now, months after that incident, Dirk lay awake in bed again. So much had changed since then, but the moffen were still the enemy. "I won't tell them who we are, Mama."

CHAPTER THIRTEEN

"DIRK! WAKE UP! Come downstairs with me." Anna stood by Dirk's bed, shaking him.

He groaned. "Just go back to sleep." He kept his eyes shut.

"But I'm hungry, and the sun's up!"

"Not so loud." He covered his ears with his hands.

She shook his arm as hard as she could. "Wake up!"

"In a little bit," he mumbled. He rolled over and pulled the blanket over his head.

A few minutes later, a pounding noise from outside woke Dirk. *Agh!* He shuffled to the window and pushed the drapes aside. The noise seemed to come from the barn. He rubbed his eyes, yawned, and turned around.

Anna's bed was empty. *No! She's probably downstairs blabbing to—*

He took the stairs two at a time, burst into the kitchen, and nearly bumped into the table. Anna was eating breakfast across the table from Colonel Fleischer. Dirk's eyes grew wide.

"Our papa is gone, but his name is—"

"Anna!" Dirk shouted.

"I was just talking to Colonel Fleischer."

Dirk's blood ran cold. He realized what had bothered him when they were introduced to Fleischer. *Fleischer* was the German word for "butcher"!

"Don't talk to people you don't know unless I'm with you," he said to Anna. "Are you done eating?"

"Uh-huh. Aren't you going to eat?"

"I'm not hungry right now. Let's go back to our room."

Colonel Fleischer set down his spoon. "You have nothing to fear from me, Dirk," he said with a tinge of irritation. "I am done fighting the war, and you have my word that I will do nothing to harm you. A German officer always keeps his word."

"Come upstairs," Dirk said to Anna, ignoring Fleischer. After they reached the bedroom, he closed the door. "Anna!" he scolded. "He said he keeps his word, but the Germans promised not to invade the Netherlands. So don't tell him anything about us or our family."

"Why? He's very nice, and he gave me chocolate." She smiled and revealed chocolate stains on her teeth.

"Agh! He's bribing you so you'll talk," Dirk said. *It's no wonder Mama warned me about him.* "It's really hard to know who you can trust during a war," he told Anna. *Oh! That's what Fleischer said yesterday.* "But you know you can trust me, and Els left me in charge of you. So don't talk to him unless I'm right by you," he ordered. "Understand?"

"Uh-huh. But if I don't talk to him, how will I get more chocolate?"

"Just don't talk to him," Dirk said.

A few minutes later, someone knocked on their bedroom door.

Dirk looked at Anna. "Remember what I told you."

"Okay."

When Dirk opened the door, Fleischer stood in the doorway with a pair of binoculars.

"What do you want?" Dirk asked.

The German brushed past Dirk and strode to the windows.

"I said, what do you want?"

He glared at Fleischer while the man scanned the roads with the binoculars. Then Fleischer strode to the window on the adjoining wall and did it again.

"As I told you, Dirk, I am done fighting the war," he finally said. "But the war is not over, and this house is in a strategic location. Because it is the only three-story building in this area, it gives an excellent vantage point for the German army to look toward the position of the Allied forces."

Uh-oh.

"There is a very good chance the German army will seize this house to use for their purposes." Fleischer rubbed his chin. "They could come as soon as tomorrow."

Dirk sat hard on the bed, as if pushed down by the weight of Fleischer's words. He'd thought the dangers were all behind him. Had he made a terrible mistake by choosing this farmhouse?

The colonel adjusted his glasses. "If they see you in those shirts, they will know you escaped from the work camp."

"We could hide in the basement," Dirk said.

"You could. But what would happen if just one soldier went down to the basement and saw you?" The question hung in the air like a large, dark cloud just before a heavy rain. Then Fleischer left the room.

Dirk paced slowly for several minutes. *Why is this happening to us?* He had led Anna to safety, and now trouble had found them again. *Or something much worse than trouble.* Even if they hid in the basement, their presence would be pretty obvious if Mrs. ten Haken kept bringing food down there. Or if Anna screamed when she saw a spider.

"Why are you wringing your hands?" Anna asked.

"I'm not wringing my ha—" He glanced down and thrust his hands into his pockets.

"Why are you walking back and forth so much? Are you worried?"

"No," he said, "I'm not worried. I'm just, I'm just, uh . . . thinking."

After a few moments, he turned to his sister. "I'm going downstairs, Anna. Stay here." Downstairs, he approached Mr. ten Haken. "Did you find any clothes for us to wear? If any German soldiers see us in our uniforms—"

"I don't have clothes your size, but anything will be better than those horrid work camp uniforms. My wife mended outfits for both of you. But you are still in danger. Any German soldiers who see you in oversize clothes will be suspicious. So you mustn't go outside for any reason. Do you understand?"

"Yes," Dirk said.

The farmer handed the clothes to him, and Dirk trudged back up the stairs to rejoin Anna. A few hours later they ate lunch with Mr. and Mrs. ten Haken. Dirk and Anna spent the afternoon in their bedroom. Anna played pretend games with the blankets, but Dirk paced and looked out the window a lot.

At supper, Dirk picked at his food. After the meal, his shoulders slumped as he plodded up the stairs to the bedroom. Several times Anna asked him to play a game, but he declined.

"But you always play with me," she protested. He didn't answer. German soldiers were probably coming soon. Tomorrow could be the worst day of their lives. *Or the last.*

At bedtime, Anna kneeled by her bed. "Dear God, help us make it to Oma and Opa's house. Tell Dirk that Colonel Fleischer is nice."

Dirk scowled, but he bent down and hugged her. "Good night, Anna."

"Tell me the Princess Anna story."

"Not tonight. I have a lot on my mind." He turned out the light and climbed into his bed, but sleep did not come for a long time.

Hours later, he woke with a start to the squeak of the door as it swung slowly open. Quiet footsteps came closer and closer.

For a few seconds, Dirk lay tensed on his back in the bed, fists clenched, heartbeat rapid, and breath shallow. *Who is it?* The visitor hid his or her face with both hands. Step, step,

step, like a slow drumbeat, the footsteps drew steadily closer. Then the intruder took two quick steps forward and lunged onto Dirk.

"Oof," he grunted as he felt the crushing weight of the assailant on his abdomen. The aggressor sat up on Dirk's stomach, leaned forward, and pinned Dirk's arms against the mattress. At close range, he got a clear view of his attacker's face.

"Get off me, Fleischer, you butcher!" Dirk shouted.

"Dirk!" Anna screamed from the other side of the room.

For one second, Dirk felt the cold flash of terror that surges through a young rabbit pinned beneath a fox. And then the feeling left, displaced by the survival instinct and a grim determination to fight. He would do more than keep family secrets from Fleischer. He would fight him. *And beat him.*

Fleischer increased his advantage by moving up to sit on the lower edge of Dirk's rib cage. He put more pressure on Dirk's arms. Dirk pushed and pulled with all his strength but couldn't move his arms at all. His face grew hot with exertion. Fleischer had the advantage of size and position. Dirk thrashed his legs, but the heavy blankets confined his movement.

"I know who your father is!" Fleischer gloated. "A so-called hero of the Dutch Resistance, but he's a coward! Why doesn't he show himself? He dares to defy the Third Reich by hiding Jews and American pilots who have been shot down. You'll pay for what your father has done."

This scoundrel insulted Papa, who was a better man than Fleischer would ever be. Dirk struggled with renewed energy but couldn't free himself from the German's iron grip. Dirk and Papa had often wrestled playfully, and his father, a champion wrestler in his youth, had told him many times, "Watch for a mistake. Then strike hard and fast." But how could he defeat an enemy so much bigger and stronger? Dirk tried to free his arms using a back-and-forth sawing motion, but he still couldn't get free.

"Look at my uniform!" Fleischer demanded. "See the eagle pin on my chest? I am the eagle, and you are a helpless field mouse." He underscored his statement by squeezing Dirk's elbows hard.

"Agh!" Dirk cried. A thunderbolt of pain shot down both forearms.

"Anna. Get Mr. ten Haken!" Dirk gasped.

"I'm scared, Dirk."

Fleischer's large hands were now past Dirk's biceps and near his shoulders. Dirk thrashed his legs again, but the effort was still ineffective.

Fleischer steadily moved his hands higher, closer to Dirk's throat. "Too bad your father isn't here to help you." He slowed his speech to savor each syllable. "And Papa's little boy has to pay for what Papa did."

Fleischer slid his grip several centimeters higher, almost to Dirk's throat. But with Fleischer's hands between Dirk's shoulder and his neck, Dirk's hands were free. He had one chance to make a move. It had to be the right one.

CHAPTER FOURTEEN

THIS IS FOR PAPA! Dirk slammed both fists into Fleischer's stomach.

"Ugh!" The older man grunted in pain and released his grip. Dirk followed the shot to the abdomen by punching his adversary's shoulders, which made Fleischer sit up.

"Get off!" Dirk roared. He grabbed Fleischer by the collar. Dirk pulled down hard and twisted to the right, which made the colonel roll over and land with a thud on the wood floor. Dirk scrambled out of the other side of the bed and dashed around it to face his enemy, who was already on his feet. Dirk shot a look over his shoulder at Anna. She lay on her bed with the blanket pulled up to her chin. Her eyes, wide with fear, darted back and forth between Dirk and Fleischer. Her mouth hung open in terror.

"Stay where you are, Anna, so I can protect you!" Dirk said. He snarled at his enemy. "Get out!" Dirk bent his knees, leaned forward, and put his arms slightly in front of him.

"Leave my brother alone!" Anna shrieked.

"I'm going to finish what I started," Fleischer said with quiet anger. "A German officer always keeps his word." He advanced steadily.

"Come and get me," Dirk said with a steely gaze.

When Fleischer was within striking range, Dirk threw a punch with his left arm, aimed at his antagonist's neck, which the German easily blocked by raising his right arm.

Dirk surged forward and slammed his shoulder into his adversary's exposed rib cage. He stepped back, but Fleischer was nowhere to be seen. Instead, a large dresser loomed in front of him. It had a broken knob, and Dirk's shoulder throbbed. *Huh?*

"What was that noise?" Anna asked. She yawned. "What are you doing?"

"I was . . ." He looked around the room. The bedroom door was still shut. Anna rubbed her eyes drowsily.

"It's all right," he said. He rubbed his shoulder and winced. "I, uh . . . just bumped into the dresser." *Another dream warning about Fleischer.*

He walked to his bed, lay down, adjusted the blankets, and forced himself to close his eyes.

● ● ●

"Get up! Get up!" Mr. ten Haken's voice snapped Dirk out of a deep sleep. The farmer was standing in the bedroom doorway. "German soldiers are here! Hurry! Hide in the basement!"

Dirk jumped out of bed and dashed to Anna. He scooped her up and put her head on his shoulder.

"What's going to happen?" she said. Her lower lip trembled.

"Uh, we'll be fine in the basement," he said without looking at her. He followed close behind Mr. ten Haken as they hustled down the stairs.

"Hurry!" Mr. ten Haken said. "If they see you, they'll shoot us all for hiding you." When they reached the main floor, Dirk heard men's voices outside the house.

They scurried through the kitchen, Anna clinging to Dirk. German soldiers passed by the window with their backs to him, and his heart leaped in his throat. *Don't turn around!* Hurrying down the stairs, Dirk cringed when a few steps creaked. When they reached the basement, he heaved a sigh of relief.

"You're not safe yet. Over here," Mr. ten Haken said. He pointed to a cellar, a wood-paneled room in the corner of the basement.

Dirk's eyebrows shot up. "What about our beds? It'll be obvious someone slept in them."

"My wife's taking care of that. Now you stay quiet and stay in the cellar, because there's no mercy for anyone who hides Jews or escapees."

"Wait!" Dirk said. "Where's Colonel Fleischer?"

"He's outside giving the soldiers orders to bring in their supplies. Either he lied to us about leaving the army, or he really did, and these soldiers don't know it yet. But they're sure to find out soon, and when they do, it will be bad for him *and* for you." Mr. ten Haken left, closing the door behind him.

Dirk glared at the closed cellar door. "Fleischer lied! He said he wouldn't fight anymore. But now he's helping

German soldiers. 'A German officer always keeps his word.' Ha!" Now Fleischer's true intent was obvious. The monkey had definitely come out of the sleeve. Dirk rubbed his chin. Those dreams had to be warnings about Fleischer.

Since Fleischer couldn't be trusted, Dirk and Anna would have to escape. They'd escaped from the gun factory, and they'd get out of here, too. Dirk turned to take stock of the room. All four cellar walls had empty shelves. Daylight trickled in through a dirty window about two meters above the floor and partially illuminated the two-meter by three-meter room.

Dirk studied the window, about half a meter long on each side. He put his hands on his hips; then he kept the distance between his hands the same while he raised them toward the window. He smiled.

"Anna. I'll be right back."

"Where are you going?"

"I'm getting something we need," he said.

He opened the cellar door cautiously and looked in all directions before he made his move. He grabbed a chair near the workbench on the other side of the basement and set it under the cellar window. He stood on the chair but couldn't reach the top of the window, where the latch was. He frowned. If he couldn't open the window, they would be at the mercy of any nosy soldier who came down to the basement.

Dirk stepped down from the chair and kicked the wall in frustration. In the process, he lost his balance and steadied himself by putting his foot on one of the shelves built into the cellar wall. He stared at the shelf.

"What are you looking at?" Anna asked.

"Watch," he said. He climbed the shelves on the wall containing the window until he reached the window latch. It stuck initially but opened with a second effort. He looked at the window and then at his shoulders, then closed the window and climbed down.

Dirk smiled. *We'll sneak out right under the Nazis' noses.*

"What are you doing?" Anna asked.

"We're getting out of here. Fleischer thinks we're trapped, but tonight we'll climb the shelves and go out the window."

Anna looked at the shelves and the window doubtfully.

A little before noon, Mrs. ten Haken came down to the basement with a large basket. She handed blankets to Dirk and Anna from the top of the basket and gave them bread and cups of water from the bottom. Her face was drawn, and she looked over her shoulder several times as she spoke to them.

"Make the bread last," she said. "I can't spare any more for you today. The soldiers are eating everything I have." She wrung her hands.

"Thank you," Dirk said.

"You're welcome," she said as she left.

Dirk divided the bread into two piles. "This pile is for now," he told Anna, pointing to the slices he had put on the chair. "That pile is for later." He nodded toward the food he had placed on the top shelf. "Do you understand?"

"Uh-huh."

After they ate, Dirk said, "We won't get much sleep tonight, so we should both take a nap." He lay down on the floor and motioned to Anna to come to him. After she sat next to him, he leaned her toward him and steered her head toward his stomach. After they rested, they spent the rest of the afternoon talking, practicing climbing the shelves, and waiting for darkness.

Late in the afternoon, Mrs. ten Haken brought a pitcher of water.

"Thank you," Dirk and Anna said.

"I wish I could do more for you." She reached out and smoothed Anna's hair. Then she left.

Anna sipped her water.

"Do you remember what I told you about tonight?" Dirk asked.

"Uh-huh. We're going to escape, right?" Anna asked.

"Yes."

"But the soldiers will see us."

"Not if we're really careful," he answered.

"Are you sure?" she asked.

"Yes," he said. His right hand twitched, and he pushed it into his pocket. When he felt the small stone, his hand quieted.

"But how can you be sure?" Anna asked.

"Because it's a good plan." *I hope.*

Thirty minutes later, three sharp knocks on the cellar door startled Dirk. *I didn't hear anyone come down the steps. Who would sneak down now?*

"Is it a soldier?" Anna whispered. She scurried behind Dirk. He grabbed the chair and held it in front of him, with the legs pointed away, and practiced a couple of thrusts. *But what can a chair do against an armed soldier?*

The door eased open. Fleischer stood in the doorway.

"Sooner or later one of the soldiers will find you." He strode into the room and looked at Anna. "One of you will make a noise." Dirk set the chair down. "Or the farmer and his wife will let something slip in conversation. If I try to protect you, they'll think I'm a traitor."

"You said you were done fighting the war," Dirk said. "You lied! And you brought those soldiers here!" Lying was bad enough, but now Fleischer acted like he was trying to help.

"I didn't lie, and I didn't bring the soldiers here." He paused. "I am done with the war, but the war is not done with me. War is bigger than you or I and even bigger than nations."

Dirk glared at Fleischer. "Another thing. If you really deserted the army, why aren't the soldiers arresting you?"

"My superiors gave me permission to visit my family. That's where they think I am, so no one will report me as absent without leave."

"I don't believe you," Dirk said.

"Of course you don't." Fleischer shook his head. "You are only a child, and you don't understand."

"I'm not a child," Dirk said through clenched teeth. "I'm thirteen."

Fleischer held up his hand. "There is more. The German army will probably use this house as a forward observation post."

"So?"

"When the Wehrmacht hurls its shells at the American army, the soldiers upstairs will report on their accuracy so the gunners can adjust their aim." Fleischer walked to the cellar window. "The Allies will discover that, and they'll smash the house with their bombers like a sledgehammer would crush a cup." He pounded his right fist into his left palm.

"What are we going to do?" Anna asked, looking up at Dirk. He didn't answer.

After an uncomfortable silence, Fleischer spoke again. "You are too quiet, which means you are thinking." He looked around the cellar and stepped toward the shelves. He reached out and traced the outline of a shoe print on a waist-high shelf.

"Ah. You were planning to climb the shelves and crawl out the window," he said. He stroked his chin. "You thought you'd leave tonight and walk to the Allied lines." Fleischer shook his head. "It won't work. It'll be below freezing, you don't have coats, and Anna could never walk the thirteen kilometers from here to Nijmegen. Even if you had a bicycle with a basket big enough to carry Anna, you'd never get through the German checkpoint before you get to the Allied lines. Your father is a Dutch national hero, and if they got any idea of who you are, you would be very valuable hostages."

"You don't know anything about my father," Dirk shot back. *In my dream he said he knew about Papa, but this is real life. He's bluffing.* He furrowed his forehead.

"As a German officer, I know about our enemies, and that means I know a great deal about your father," Fleischer said. "Hans Ingelse is a hero to the Dutch."

"You know our papa?" Anna asked.

"Stay out of this, Anna," Dirk snapped.

"I've read his complete file, which includes pictures of both of you." Fleischer paused. "Your father is a leader of the Dutch Resistance."

"He's what?" Anna said.

"Anna!" Dirk scolded. He turned back to Fleischer, crossed his arms, and glared.

"Three years ago, he and others persuaded Dutch workers to go on strike to protest the deportation of Jews." Dirk's eyes grew wide. "Later," Fleischer continued, "your father oversaw smuggling Jewish children out of a holding center. Volunteers passed them over a hedge, carried them into a neighboring school, hid them in baskets, and cycled them to the countryside, where other volunteers cared for the youngsters. But I didn't come down here to talk about your father."

While Fleischer talked, Dirk stared at the eagle pin on the German's uniform. In Dirk's dream, Fleischer had made a big deal about the eagle, and its wings had been turned up at the ends. *But Fleischer's eagle's wings go straight across. Why is it different? Is that part of the warning?*

"I have told the soldiers and Mr. and Mrs. ten Haken of the danger they face from the impending bombing attack. Now you know too." Then Fleischer left.

CHAPTER FIFTEEN

"Agh!" Dirk's shoulders sagged. "We can't stay here, and we can't go to the Allied lines."

"What are we going to do?" Anna asked.

"I don't know. Papa would know what to do."

"He would say, 'Keep your hopes up and your prayers strong,'" Anna said.

"I know. Els said that too." Dirk sighed. All his life he had dreamed of saving the day. But in his flights of fancy it was never this hard. Dirk backed up to the cellar wall and slid to a seated position on the floor. Anna nestled against his side.

He draped his arm around her shoulder. "I'll think of something. We'll get out of here." *I wish I could ask Papa what to do.*

A memory flashed. Two years earlier, he had asked Papa about a classmate. A year older than Dirk, Franz had insulted, threatened, and punched Dirk nearly every day. Dirk and Papa reported Franz to the head of the school, but despite his promise to look into it, nothing changed.

"The answer to the problem is in the problem," Papa said one day when Dirk came home with bruises on his arms. Dirk wrinkled his nose and stared at his father.

"The problem is that he's bigger and stronger and probably overconfident," Papa said. "Use that to beat him." They talked a bit more, and Papa showed Dirk a few special wrestling moves.

The next day after school, Franz followed Dirk down an alley when no one else was around. Dirk couldn't outrun the other boy, so he turned and faced him.

Now as Dirk sat on the cellar floor, his pulse quickened as he recalled the confrontation. He'd looked Franz in the eye and said, "Quit bothering me!"

"You think you're so much better than me, Dutchie boy." Franz was of German descent and never missed a chance to taunt his Dutch peers. "What's the matter, Dirk? Why don't you say something? What's the matter?" He shoved him hard. "Is your mouth full of teeth?"

"No, I'm not at a loss for words. Just leave me alone, Franz!"

Franz reached out and squeezed Dirk's bicep. "You're weak, just like the Netherlands. When the war started, you and your army lasted *five whole days*. Oh! I don't know how you did it."

"Go away, Franz."

"I will after I've taught you a lesson, Dutchie." Franz charged at Dirk. Dirk let him lunge, then stepped aside. The moment Franz righted himself, Dirk backed into him, and grabbing Franz's arm, he flipped him onto the ground. *Thanks, Papa.*

Franz rushed Dirk three more times and ended up on the

ground each time. Franz finally stood and brushed off his shirt. Breathing hard, he said, "You're nothing but a coward, Dutchie! You're too scared to fight with your fists." But he never bothered Dirk again.

Dirk stood in the middle of the cellar and looked at the dirty window. "So the problem is that we'll die if we stay and die if we walk out of here," he muttered to himself. "What else is there? If the answer is in the problem, then where's the answer?"

He closed his eyes and rubbed his temples. All his efforts to keep Anna safe would come to nothing if Fleischer was right about the soldiers.

"Dear God, help us get out of here. Amen," Anna said behind him.

Dirk snapped his fingers.

"Why did you do that?" Anna asked.

He beamed at her. "We're getting out of here."

"I know. We're going to sneak out the window after dark."

"That's not what I mean. I'm going to use Papa's advice."

"What?"

The door at the top of the stairs opened, and Dirk and Anna tensed as they listened for footsteps. Opening the cellar door a crack, Dirk held his breath and peeked out. Mr. ten Haken reached the basement and grabbed a few tools from the workbench. *Whew! It's not a soldier!*

Dirk approached the farmer. "Would you please tell Colonel Fleischer I need to see him?"

"Why?" Mr. ten Haken asked. "Nothing good can come from talking to a man like that."

"I have to ask him something," Dirk said. He stood still, his eyes slightly squinted in concentration.

Mr. ten Haken pursed his lips. "All right." He waved a finger. "I'll tell him, but I'm warning you, he's still the enemy."

"Why do you want to talk to Colonel Fleischer?" Anna asked after Mr. ten Haken went back upstairs. "I thought you didn't trust him."

"I don't. But sometimes you have to take a chance, because it's the only chance you have," Dirk said.

"Huh?" Anna said.

"Just watch," he said. "And let me do the talking."

A few minutes later, Colonel Fleischer came down to the cellar.

"Colonel, Anna and I need your help." Dirk's voice quavered. "We need you to drive us to the Allied lines in Nijmegen."

Fleischer snorted. "Since when does a German officer take orders from a young boy?"

"Let me finish," Dirk said. His right hand shook, and he shoved it into his pocket. "If you go back to the German army, you'll be shot for deserting. You said anyone who stays here will die from a bombing attack. So if you can't go back and you can't stay here, the only thing left is for you to go forward."

"What?"

"We can't get through the German checkpoint to the Allied lines without you, and you need us, too. When you deliver two children of a Dutch hero, you'll be treated well by the Allies."

Fleischer smirked. "Clever of you to ask a favor and make

it sound like my idea." He stared straight ahead, his grim expression unchanging, for about thirty seconds. Fleischer removed his officer's hat and ran a hand through his thinning hair. He took a deep breath and replaced his hat. "I will consider it," he said, then went back upstairs without another word.

Dirk paced the cellar. What would Fleischer say? If he said no, the only option would be to escape through the window, but Fleischer was right. Anna wouldn't be able to walk all the way to Nijmegen, and Dirk couldn't carry her the whole way either. Dirk grunted. Fleischer was their only chance. He *had* to say yes.

Fifteen minutes later the basement stairs creaked. "Here comes our only hope," Dirk said under his breath. When the colonel reached the cellar, he looked Dirk in the eye for several seconds. Dirk bit his lip and waited.

"Your idea has merit." Fleischer paused. "I will drive you to Nijmegen. You are like your father, Dirk. They say he can talk almost anyone into nearly anything."

Dirk jumped and threw his hands in the air in victory— and hit them on the ceiling. He rubbed the back of his hands, but his smile did not dim. They would finally get to the American army base, and then no Nazis could touch them! Weeks of life-and-death decisions would be behind him, and then they'd go look for Papa!

"I told you Colonel Fleischer was nice," Anna said.

Even then Dirk kept smiling. She could say anything about Fleischer, and it wouldn't spoil Dirk's mood.

"I'll come for you tomorrow night," Fleischer said,

snapping Dirk back to the present. "The German army will have extra patrols on the road to Nijmegen tonight, so we'll have to wait. Tomorrow evening, I'll take you to the barn, and you will wait there until I come for you in the middle of the night." Fleischer paused. "There are several ways this plan could go wrong and we could all die."

CHAPTER SIXTEEN

NOVEMBER 25

THE NEXT DAY, shortly before sunset, Fleischer appeared at the cellar doorway. "It's time to go to the barn."

"I didn't hear you come down," Dirk said.

"Neither did anyone else. Now be quick and be quiet. Don't talk, sneeze, or cough. No sound. The soldiers are outside, on the other side of the house. When I tell you, run!"

Fleischer led them up the stairs and to the back door. Dirk put a finger to his lips to remind Anna to be quiet. But if something startled her, she would cry out despite her good intentions. "Go!" Fleischer whispered, and Dirk and Anna scurried toward the barn. Nerves on edge, looking and listening intently for soldiers, Dirk heard every little sound—the *swish, swish* of his trousers, the breeze in his ears. And in spite of himself, he nearly cried out in surprise when a bird swooped by on its way into the barn.

In the barn, Fleischer spoke again. "Talk softly, don't make any loud noises, and after the sun goes down, get some sleep. It will be quite a while before we go, and you'll need your rest because it could be a difficult night. Find a spot where you can't be seen from the door. I'm going back into the house."

Dirk nodded and led Anna behind a pile of hay bales six meters from the door. He turned around and sized up their position. The single bulb above the doorway would give him a good view of anyone entering after dark, but by that time, he and Anna would be in deep shadows behind the hay. No one would see them unless they did a thorough search of the barn. *Which a squad of soldiers could do.* The barn suddenly felt chillier.

"Dirk!" Anna said. "Look!" Her arm trembled as she pointed up.

"Shh!" he scolded. He cringed and looked toward the house. "You can't make noise, Anna. Soldiers might hear you."

He followed Anna's gaze toward the barn ceiling. A cat in the rafters stalked a barn swallow with an injured wing.

"The cat's going to get the bird," Anna whispered. She turned her head and shut her eyes. Dirk picked a small rock off the barn floor, cocked his arm, then dropped the rock.

"Why aren't you—?"

"The bird's not really hurt."

"But you have to do something!"

"No, Anna. The bird's playing a trick on the cat."

"What?"

"The cat got close to a nest of baby birds, so the mama's pretending to be injured to lure the cat away from her nest."

A minute later, the bird flew away and perched on a higher rafter.

"See?" Dirk said. "The barn swallow is okay, the baby birds in the nest are safe, and the mother will fly back to them when the cat's not looking."

"Oh," Anna said. "That scared me."

"It's okay," he said. He patted her on the shoulder. "We should sleep."

"But I can't sleep. I'm cold."

"Take your arms out of your sleeves and fold them over your stomach inside your shirt. That will make you warmer," Dirk said. He put his arm around her. She leaned her head against his shoulder and closed her eyes.

"Does that feel warmer now?"

"Uh-huh."

Dirk lay awake for some time, listening to Anna's breathing. As hard as the past weeks had been, it felt good to be her protector.

"This time tomorrow we'll be safe at Oma and Opa's house," he whispered to himself. "Or," his voice choked up, "if Fleischer's leading us into a trap, we'll be dead."

He adjusted his blankets and waited for drowsiness to come. He looked down at Anna, snuggled against his side, to be sure she was asleep. He bowed his head. "Help us get to Oma and Opa's house, and protect Papa and Els," he whispered. *I prayed again. Anna's getting to me.* He smiled.

Dirk thought back to a time when Els had watched over him, like he was watching over Anna now. When Dirk was six years old, one day on his way home from school, he'd thought it would be fun to walk on the edge of a canal. When he stumbled over a stone, Els caught his flailing hand and pulled him away from the edge.

Dirk was older now, and he had to help Els by finding Papa. But first he and Anna had to get to Oma and Opa's house.

He closed his eyes and sighed. "Good night, Papa and Els, wherever you are." His breathing slowed.

Dirk woke when the large barn door slid open. He cupped his hand behind his ear and held his breath. *What if it's not Fleischer?* His pulse quickened, and he clenched his fists.

"Dirk," a male voice whispered.

Dirk stood up halfway and eased his eyes over the hay bales in front of him. Spotting Fleischer, he stepped from behind the hay bales. "Over here, Colonel."

"I sent the guard inside and told him I would stand watch for him for a few minutes," Fleischer said. "We don't have much time. We'll push the car out to the road and drive away."

Dirk scooped up Anna, still asleep, and moved toward the car.

"Have you ever driven a car?" Fleischer asked.

"No, but I've driven the tractor and truck on our farm many times."

"Good. You'll drive, then," Fleischer said.

"Why?"

"So I can shoot."

Dirk flinched. "Who would you shoot at?"

"In case a problem develops at the checkpoint, I need to be ready."

"But would you really shoot German soldiers?"

"I'd rather not, but I'll do what I have to do."

So Dirk's worries weren't over. It sounded like Fleischer wasn't sure how it would go. Dirk carried Anna to the car. She stirred a bit as he set her down but didn't waken. He placed her on the floor just behind the front seat, with a blanket over her. If there was any shooting, she'd be a little safer there. Fleischer checked his pistol. Dirk shivered, and not just due to the chilly air.

"Hurry," Fleischer said. "The guard will come outside soon."

Following Fleischer's instructions, Dirk put both hands on the back right corner of the car. Fleischer put one hand on the window frame and the other on the steering wheel.

"Push," he ordered. The car rolled quietly out of the barn. As it approached the road, Fleischer turned the steering wheel.

"Stop," he said. As the car slowed, he opened the door, stepped on the brake, set the parking brake, and hurried around to the passenger side of the car.

"Get in!" He waved at Dirk to hurry to the driver's seat. They quickly climbed into the car, Fleischer in the back, next to Anna, and Dirk in the driver's seat. He took a moment to look at the controls and pedals.

"Start the car!" Fleischer said. "We don't have time!"

Dirk turned the key, but nothing happened. He looked helplessly at Fleischer.

"*Dummkopf!*" the German hissed. "Push the clutch down."

"Oh." Dirk pushed the clutch down and turned the key, and the engine started normally.

"Drive!" Fleischer said, nostrils flaring. He glanced over his shoulder toward the house. "Hurry!" Dirk released the clutch, and the car moved forward.

"Take it up to twenty kilometers per hour and keep it there," Fleischer said. "You'll need to go slowly because we have to keep the headlights off."

"We should have escaped during the day when we could see better," he told Fleischer.

"No. Allied fighter pilots would see us, and they would love to shoot a German officer's car."

Dirk leaned forward and strained to see the road ahead. Clouds blocked most of the moonlight. They drove in silence for a minute as Anna slept in the back seat.

"Roll your window down a few centimeters," Fleischer ordered. He did the same with his. "Listen for sounds outside the car."

"What am I listening for?" Dirk asked as he lowered his window.

"Anything, but especially gunfire."

Gunfire? Was there something Fleischer wasn't telling Dirk?

Dirk gripped the steering wheel more tightly. Hopefully Fleischer could talk his way through the checkpoint, but if not, what would happen? Their odds were not good—all of those soldiers with their guns against Fleischer with only a pistol. So this was why he had said they could all die. Dirk's blood ran cold.

"Five minutes to the checkpoint. Maybe less," Fleischer said.

"What are you going to tell the guards at the checkpoint?" Dirk asked.

"I'll tell them the German high command authorized an exchange—Anna for the son of a German general," Fleischer said.

Dirk narrowed his eyes. Why had he trusted Fleischer? He had said German officers keep their word, but he'd lied to his superiors about where he was, and now he would lie to the guards at the checkpoint to get them all through. And Dirk's life and Anna's were in this man's hands.

Dirk's heart sank. But it was too late to change his mind now. That bullet had already passed through the church. He squirmed in the driver's seat.

"Tell me if you see or hear anything," Fleischer ordered.

"I will."

"If something goes wrong and they start shooting, you have to drive fast right away and keep driving no matter what. Even if I am wounded, keep driving!"

"I understand," Dirk said. He furrowed his forehead in concentration. If something went wrong at the checkpoint, the soldiers would have the advantage of numbers and weapons. He and Fleischer needed some kind of advantage. But what? If only they had a secret weapon. Dirk tapped his fingers on the steering wheel—and then he smiled.

Fleischer tightened his grip on his pistol and rolled his

window all the way down. More chilly air blew in. He pressed his lips tightly together, leaned toward the window, and strained his eyes and ears.

"There it is," Fleischer said. "Put my hat on," he said, handing it up from the back seat to Dirk, "and don't let them see your face. They have to think you're my driver for this to work."

"I understand," Dirk said again. He put on the hat, took his foot off the gas pedal, lightly touched the brakes as they approached the checkpoint, and thought over his secret strategy one more time.

CHAPTER SEVENTEEN

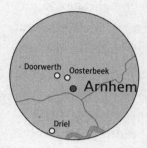

GESTAPO INTERROGATION CENTER
OOSTERBEEK
NOVEMBER 22

"Don't go to sleep tonight," a guard told Els. "You'll be questioned at eleven o'clock."

After he left, Els sat with the bright overhead light still on and guards making plenty of noise to be sure she couldn't sleep. They kept up the racket until many hours later when a different guard entered her cell and informed her the appointment had been postponed.

Two nights later, the Germans told her she must stay awake and await questioning at midnight. Shortly after the three o'clock shift change, they told her she could go to sleep. Immediately, she grabbed her little heart of stone from the corner where she'd hidden it, curled up on the mattress, and slept.

The next morning they questioned her without warning before breakfast, but she told them nothing. That afternoon, they took her to a room with a bar on the wall high above her head. They tied her hands together and connected them to a rope, which they looped around the bar. After an hour, Els's arms ached and throbbed. Just when she thought she couldn't take it anymore, a guard brought a plate of bratwurst and sauerkraut and set it on a table along with a glass of water. "Here is your dinner," he said. Els's mouth watered, her nose twitched, and she couldn't take her eyes off the food.

"Hey!" Els yelled at him as he left. "You forgot to untie me!"

The man stepped toward Els. "No. I didn't forget." A few minutes later he returned with a chair. "It's too bad you didn't want your food." He held the plate to his nose and inhaled deeply with his eyes closed. "Ahhh." He twirled the fork as he chewed, eyes locked on Els's. She returned his stare, keeping her face as blank as she could. After he left, Els's arms ached and her stomach growled.

With her arms still trapped in the air, her mind went to work. In the first few days after Els's arrest, she had focused on not breaking under pressure and talking about Papa. But now a new fear largely replaced the first one, like a cold, chilling fog that pushed out a previous weather system. Now Els feared she wouldn't make it out of this prison alive. Would she die of disease due to poor nourishment? Or would they execute her for not talking? She grimaced. The Gestapo's prisoners often melted into what the enemy called "night and fog." Perhaps Els and the other prisoners here were just phantoms waiting to die.

Els should have seen her arrest coming. When Mama died, something inside her had snapped. Mama's passing wasn't directly the Nazis' fault, but Els had decided to take out her feelings of loss and anger on the enemy. By day she worked in the permit department of the city government so she could pay the bills, but by night she gave herself to Resistance activities. At the time, Els saw their activities as a heroic struggle against a mighty enemy that the Dutch were certain to eventually defeat.

But not now. Els's body was gaunt, and her filthy hair was matted. Now she saw the war as a grim struggle to survive against an enemy who wanted to choke the life out of her country—and out of Els. Every day the starvation diet and harsh treatment sapped her strength. As she stood now with her arms above her head for what must have been hours but felt even longer, her arms and legs screamed for relief. "Ohh," she moaned.

A guard entered the room. He untied her hands, and her arms collapsed to her sides. He ordered her to a room where a cigar-smoking interrogator motioned for her to sit. Exhausted, she fell into the chair.

The questions weren't new, but the fact that the man blew smoke in Els's face throughout the long conversation made it much more stressful. Both of her hands were unbound on the table in front of her, and she waved at the smoke to clear the air, but in spite of that, she soon coughed and her eyes burned. For the hundredth time, the man inhaled deeply on his cigar, the tip glowing bright red. A moment later, he exhaled and suddenly jabbed the cigar down on the back of Els's hand.

She screamed as she yanked her hand back. Pain shot up

her arm. She rubbed and squeezed the forearm of the injured hand to try to distract herself from the unbearable burning sensation.

"Maybe now you'd like to talk," the interrogator said to Els.

She doubled over in pain, cradling her burned hand in her lap. "Ohh, ohh," she said as she rocked back and forth. Tears sprang from her eyes. She hung her head and wiped both eyes with her uninjured hand. She grimaced in pain again and hugged herself as if that were the only comfort she could get. She gave a small nod. "I—I would like to talk," she whispered. "I will tell you everything you want to know."

The interrogator smiled and poised his pen. Els looked down at the floor and then up at the man again. Suddenly she sat up straight. She took a moment to gather her strength and savor what she was about to say. "I will tell you everything you want to know," she said, with eyes narrowed and voice determined, "as soon as you have been convicted of war crimes and the whole world knows the awful things you have—"

"Silence!" he roared. "How dare you lecture me! Guard! Cut her rations in half!" Turning back to Els, he snarled, "Soon your empty stomach will make you talk." He stormed out of the room, and a guard took Els back to her cell.

Weak with fatigue and hunger, Els fetched the pebble from the corner of her cell. She normally only held the little stone overnight, but she needed to feel it now. She needed what it had come to mean to her. After a while, she tucked it into her shoe to hide it from the Nazis.

Just before bedtime another interrogator visited her.

"Since you won't talk, interrogations are over. There is no further chance of mercy from the Gestapo. All that remains is for you to be sentenced."

He moved Els to a smaller cell. The walls were covered with writing. She read, "Jacobus is the son of Gerrit. Cornelia is the wife of Petrus." Some fifty people had scratched their names into the concrete, leaving a mark to prove they'd been there. *And they mattered.* Els felt a lump in her throat. Where were these people now? The last message read, "I defy Hitler," but the name was obscured by a large, head-high bloodstain.

The next day, in the early afternoon, a guard charged into Els's cell. He pointed the bayonet on his rifle toward the hall. Something in the guard's facial expression told her she wouldn't be returning to the cell. Ever. She feigned rising to her feet but collapsed with a loud groan, her hand covering the stone in the corner of her cell. Then she doubled over with a long, hacking cough, putting her hand over her mouth and slipping the pebble under her tongue. Finally, despite being weak with hunger, Els willed herself to a standing position. "Where are you taking me?" she asked.

"Your sentence has been determined," he said.

Wrapping her tattered blanket around her shoulders, Els trudged down the hall, following other prisoners also being moved. Outside, the stiff, chilly breeze flapped her blanket, and she clutched it tighter around her. Guards formed the captives in a row, spaced one meter apart in front of a brick wall. More guards stood on the opposite side of the small fenced yard with rifles.

"Nooo!" cried a man next to Els. "They're going to—"

"*Halt die Klappe!*" a soldier shouted. A light rain fell. Els put her hand on the shoulder of the man who had cried out. His weeping intensified to wailing. "Nooo!" he cried, turning one way and another as if appealing to some unseen authority.

"All of you are guilty of crimes against the Third Reich," an officer announced. "You have been sentenced, and now you will pay for what you have done."

He looked at the soldiers. "Ready," he shouted above the din of prisoners begging for mercy. The soldiers clutched their rifles.

With her tongue, Els maneuvered the small stone in her mouth between her tongue and cheek so she could project her voice. She cleared her throat, and she sang as loudly as she could in her weakened condition, "Grant that I may remain brave, your servant for always," she began. Several prisoners joined her in singing the national anthem. "And may defeat the tyranny which pierces my heart."

"Wait!" the man next to Els cried, looking at the officer. "I'll talk. I want to see my family again!" Stretching his arms in front of him, the bedraggled man slowly approached the officer. When he got within two meters of the German, he stopped. "Pleeeeease," he begged, then his words dissolved into sobbing.

"Take him inside. If he lies or won't answer a question, you know what to do."

A soldier led the man away. In the pause that followed, some prisoners screamed, others wept openly, and some said nothing.

"Ready!" the officer shouted again.

Thunder boomed, and the rain fell harder. It wasn't supposed to end like this. The Gestapo was supposed to realize Els would never talk, and they'd let her go. And then she'd somehow find Dirk and Anna.

"Aim," the officer said. The soldiers raised their rifles.

Els clenched her teeth. They could take her life but not her spirit. She ran her tongue over the smooth surface of the stone in her mouth. With her eyes fixed on the soldiers, she raised her right hand to her forehead in a farewell salute to her family. *Goodbye, Papa. Be safe, Anna and Dirk. Keep your hopes up and—*

"Put your weapons down," the officer ordered the soldiers. "Let this be a lesson," he said to the prisoners. "Your life is completely in our hands. If you had simply answered our questions, you would have been set free to rejoin your families. But instead, where I send you, you will be at the mercy of new interrogators, whose methods are, shall we say, very effective." He turned back to the soldiers. "Take them away!"

As soldiers led them through a gate, Els's mind raced. She'd been delivered from death, but what lay ahead? Nothing the moffen had in mind for her could be good. Her legs trembled as rifle butts and curses herded her and the other prisoners into the back of a Gestapo van. Unseen hands slammed the back door and locked it with a metallic clank.

The captives collapsed on the floor from physical and mental fatigue, but they soon found their voices. One man said that because his family had hidden Jews, soldiers gave them only twenty minutes to gather a few essentials before being taken into captivity. In addition, the Nazis gave their house away to new residents and ordered the man's children to arrange bouquets of flowers for the newcomers. A murmur of sympathy rippled through the group.

A woman said the Gestapo had arrested her for naming her pig Hitler. With voices hoarse due to their emaciated condition, the captives howled with glee, and happy tears flowed. When the merriment ebbed, someone said, "I bet your pig had better manners than Herr Hitler," and the laughter exploded again.

"And I bet the pig had a better mustache, too," Els added. She laughed so hard her sides soon hurt. It was good to feel human again.

Minutes later the van stopped, and the door swung open. Rain still poured down.

"Where are we?" a woman asked as she peered at a large building.

"Nowhere we want to be," Els answered. She lowered her voice. "Stay strong. And don't tell them anything." *Heart of stone.*

CHAPTER EIGHTEEN

GERMAN CHECKPOINT
NORTH OF NIJMEGEN
NOVEMBER 26

DIRK'S HEART POUNDED, and his palms grew sweaty as the checkpoint came into view. On the right stood a narrow guardhouse, about a meter taller than a grown man and with a doorway just large enough for the two soldiers who stepped out of it. A long metal bar stretched across the road, blocking traffic. On the left stood two soldiers holding rifles at waist level, pointed away from Dirk and his approaching car. *At least they're not aimed at us for now.*

"*Heil Hitler!*" Fleischer called in a formal tone to a soldier who approached the car. "I am Colonel Fleischer."

Dirk pretended to scratch his forehead with his hand to hide his youthful face from the enemy.

"I am authorized to conduct an exchange," Fleischer said. "I am bringing a young Dutch girl, who is the daughter of the mayor of Nijmegen"—he pointed to Anna, who was still

133

asleep—"across the bridge to Nijmegen in exchange for the son of General Fromm, who was captured by the Resistance."

Dirk wanted to look at the soldier's face as he listened to Fleischer. Was he believing the colonel, or was the situation about to turn deadly? But he didn't dare show that much interest or risk exposing his face.

"I'll have to check on this," the soldier said. "We've not been given any word about it. Our strict orders are to not allow *anyone* through our checkpoint during the night." He strode back to the guardhouse.

As soon as he entered the guardhouse, Fleischer spoke. "Drive now! Before they realize the story's not true," the colonel hissed.

"Not yet," Dirk said out of the side of his mouth.

A soldier on the left side of the checkpoint took several steps toward the car.

"Get your gun ready," Dirk told Fleischer.

"It's *been* ready."

A soldier stepped out of the guardhouse, moved closer to the car, and peered into the vehicle.

"Now!" Dirk said. With one hand he clenched the steering wheel and with the other he turned on the lights—*the secret weapon*! When he popped the clutch and jammed his foot on the accelerator, the engine roared, and the car leapt forward.

"What are you doing?" Anna cried, woken by the commotion.

The soldiers yelled in response to the blinding light and the car surging toward them. Fleischer stuck his gun out the window and fired in the direction of the startled Germans. The one who had been nearly in front of the car dove out of the way. Two soldiers scurried out of the car's path, shielded their eyes with one hand, and fired their guns with the other. But their shots were wild. The car crashed through the metal bar which had blocked their way.

Dirk's eyes darted back and forth between the road ahead and the speedometer. Twenty kilometers per hour. Twenty-five. If he could drive fast enough, they might make it. He'd surprised them with the headlights. Hope surged in his chest. But the enemy soldiers were still shooting, and they were close.

Anna screamed.

Fleischer shot back several times. Thirty-five kilometers per hour.

"Dirk!" Anna cried.

"Stay down!" Dirk and Fleischer said.

The gunfire continued, and at least one bullet shattered the rear passenger window.

"Dirk!" Anna shrieked.

"Are you all right?" Dirk shouted.

"I have glass all over me."

"Stay down! We're almost to the bridge."

"I'm scared!" Anna said.

Fleischer fired repeatedly in the direction of the guard-house. He reloaded, smoke from his gun swirling in the car.

Dirk shifted into third gear as more shots rang out from behind them. Fleischer shot back. Forty-five kilometers per hour.

But as the car sped forward, the bridge drew near. Dirk's

jaw dropped, and his eyes grew wide. He saw a meter-high barrier made of lumber across the entrance to the bridge. They were so close to freedom, and now this! "Nooo!" he said as he took his foot off the accelerator. "What should I do?" he shouted.

Fleischer glanced over his shoulder at the barrier. "Floor it!"

"But—"

"Do it!"

Dirk's foot hovered between the brake and gas pedal. The car slowed a bit. Shots from behind pinged off the back of the car. What should he do? The wrong choice would mean injury or death. He mashed his foot down on the accelerator.

Back up to forty kilometers per hour. Forty-five. "We're going to crash! Stay on the floor, Anna!" he shouted.

How thick was the barrier? Was this how it would end, less than two kilometers from the safety of the American army? The instant before impact, Dirk shut his eyes tight and braced himself. Fleischer covered his face with his arms. They both hollered in fear.

The sedan crashed into the wood with an explosion of noise. The car broke through the barrier, but the impact crumpled the hood, jolted the vehicle, and reduced its speed to a crawl. The sudden slowing hurled Dirk and Fleischer forward with violent force.

"Ow!" Dirk cried. His chest smashed against the steering wheel, and his forehead smacked the windshield. Jolts of pain shot through his torso and head. Everything hurt. Really hurt. He wheezed as the blow forced the air from his lungs. He opened his eyes.

"Dirk!!!" Anna wailed.

Chunks of lumber sledgehammered the hood and slammed into the windshield, which shattered, spraying Dirk's face with razor-sharp shards. Finally, the car came to a stop.

"Agh!" Dirk spit out glass and tasted blood. *Should've kept my mouth shut.*

"What happened?" Anna cried.

"Restart the car," Fleischer said as he wiped traces of blood from his lower lip. "Get your speed up again to ride over the remaining boards."

"Stay down, Anna," Dirk said as he turned the key.

The engine turned over but didn't start.

"Did we wreck the engine?" Dirk asked. He swallowed hard.

"No. Try it again!"

But when Dirk turned the key, the engine sputtered more weakly than before.

"It's not working," Dirk said. His breath came in short pants as the gunshots behind them increased.

"It has to. Try again," Fleischer said.

Bullets ricocheted off the bridge structure around the car.

As Dirk reached for the key, his right hand shook, but by an effort of will, he grabbed the key and closed his eyes. This was their last chance.

He turned the key. The engine coughed.

"Come on. Come on," Fleischer urged.

The engine sputtered.

"Push the accelerator!" Fleischer shouted.

The car started. Dirk shifted into first gear, and the car moved forward. But with the headlights broken, he strained to see the road ahead.

"Faster! And keep your head down!" Fleischer said. He fired back. "They're close now."

"I'm scared!" Anna cried.

"Stay down!" Dirk and Fleischer roared in unison.

A bullet narrowly missed Dirk and buried itself in the middle of the dashboard.

Fleischer returned fire, grunted, and clutched his left shoulder.

"Did you get hit?" Dirk asked.

"Go faster!" Fleischer urged, still gripping his shoulder.

Dirk shifted into second gear.

"Turn off the lights, so they won't have the taillights to aim at," Fleischer said.

"All right."

As they reached the halfway point of the bridge, the car suddenly slowed. "Why are you slowing down?" Fleischer asked.

"I don't know," Dirk said. "I'm still pressing down on the gas pedal. And now the steering wheel's really hard to turn."

"You probably have a flat tire in front," Fleischer said. "Keep the accelerator down."

"It's already all the way down."

"Then shift to first gear and give it a lot of gas," Fleischer replied. "They're on foot, so if you get up to twenty kilometers per hour, we'll have a chance to get out of shooting range."

Only a chance?

"*Halt!* Or I'll use my bazooka," a voice bellowed from behind.

"He's bluffing," Fleischer said.

Dirk pushed the accelerator. Twelve kilometers per hour. The shots from behind stopped, but why? Did they really have a bazooka? Were they loading it? And if a bazooka could take out a tank, what would it do to a car? Dirk gulped.

Thirteen kilometers per hour.

Something exploded to the right of the car, and Dirk flinched.

"You said he was bluffing!"

"He'll reload," Fleischer said. "Drive faster!!!"

"I'm trying!"

Fourteen kilometers per hour.

"Why aren't you shooting back?" Dirk asked.

"They can't see us. The flash of my gun would give them a target."

An explosion erupted to the left, much closer to the car. Debris blew in through Dirk's open window, and he swatted the airborne fragments away from his eyes.

"That was a lot closer!" Dirk cried.

Sixteen kilometers per hour. Seventeen. "Come on, come on!" he urged the car. Nineteen kilometers per hour. He leaned forward, as if that would increase their speed.

"Twenty kilometers per hour!" he cried.

A third explosion went off, but it was farther behind.

"Keep your speed up!" Fleischer bellowed.

The gunfire behind became less frequent, and none of the shots hit the vehicle. Then the shooting stopped.

"Is it safe now?" Anna whimpered from the back seat.

"Probably," replied Fleischer. "But stay on the floor, just in case."

Dirk's heart still thumped hard, but it slowed a little.

"Are you okay, Anna?" Dirk asked.

"I'm scared."

"We're almost to town."

"Why did you shoot at members of your own army?" Dirk asked Colonel Fleischer.

"I am an expert shot. I aimed carefully and never came close to hitting any of them. But we needed the threat of the gun to give us a chance to get through."

Anna was sitting up, and all three of them strained their eyes looking ahead in the darkness without working headlights. In the moonlight, piles of sandbags came into view. "Here is the American checkpoint," Fleischer announced.

The American army! Dirk took his foot off the gas pedal. As the engine slowed, the tension drained from Dirk.

"Halt!" a deep voice said from the darkness. Dirk stopped the car, and Fleischer set his pistol on the floor in front of him.

"We made it! We made it!" Dirk exclaimed.

CHAPTER NINETEEN

"STEP OUT OF THE CAR with your hands in the air," a stern voice said.

As Dirk, Anna, and Fleischer came out of the car, five American soldiers approached with bayonets fixed on their rifles. The blades gleamed in the spotlights.

"Don't let them stab us with those things," Anna said as she clung to Dirk.

"Don't worry, Anna. They won't."

An officer spoke from behind the protective screen of the five enlisted men. "Who are you, and why are you here?" he asked.

"I am Colonel Klaus Fleischer, and I am here to surrender. These children are Dutch citizens and wish to go to their grandparents' house here in Nijmegen. Their father is Hans Ingelse, the Resistance leader."

"If you have any weapons, take them out slowly and drop them on the ground in front of you," the officer ordered.

"My pistol is in the car," Fleischer said.

A soldier lowered his gun and approached Fleischer. "Keep your hands up," he said. He frisked Fleischer, then Anna and Dirk. He found nothing on Anna but questioned a bump in Dirk's pants pocket.

"What's this?" the soldier asked.

"My papa gave me that stone." He fished the stone out of his pocket and almost dropped it because his hand was shaking so much. "You *can't* take it away," he blurted out. "Papa sent it to me when he was away."

The soldier took the stone and turned it over in his hands. "You may keep it." He handed it back to Dirk and rejoined his companions.

Dirk looked at Fleischer. "Thank you for helping us," he whispered. "But why did you do it?"

"He's nice!" Anna said. "I keep telling you."

"Anna, I'm not as nice as you think I am, but I'm not the evil man your brother thinks I am either."

"Then why did you help us?" Dirk asked.

The American officer approached.

"If I told you," Fleischer said, barely shaking his head from side to side, "you wouldn't believe me. Your father knows why."

"How does Papa know?" Dirk asked.

The American officer led Fleischer away.

Anna tapped Dirk's arm. "What's going to happen to us?"

How would Papa know why Fleischer helped us? What is Fleischer hiding?

Anna tugged on Dirk's arm. "What's going to happen to us?"

He bent down and looked her in the eye. "We're safe now," he said with a smile.

"But I'm scared of those soldiers and their guns," she said.

"Don't worry. Those guns protect us from the Germans, and we'll ask the soldiers to take us to Oma and Opa's house. When we get there, I'll give you your orange ribbon, and you can put it in your hair if you want."

"I want it now."

"No. You'll lose it if I give it to you now," he said.

"No, I won't. It's mine and—"

"Hello," a smiling nurse said as she approached Dirk and Anna. "Put these jackets on," she told them. "We only have adult sizes, but they'll keep you warm."

"Thank you," Dirk said. "A jacket would be great. We got pretty cold on the way here."

"We'll check you for injuries and get you something to eat," the nurse said.

Anna clung to Dirk as they walked to the nurse's station. The nurse checked Anna and found the blisters on her hands from the work camp and several small bruises on her arms. She discovered Dirk had a large bruise on his forehead, multiple scratches on his face, and several small cuts on his tongue, but they were not serious.

As the nurse escorted the siblings to the mess hall, Anna relaxed her grip on Dirk's hand. While they ate, the nurse asked questions about their family and their recent experiences.

"Can you take us to Oma and Opa's house now?" Anna asked.

"Not tonight, but we'll see if the soldiers can take you after the sun comes up," the nurse replied.

As they ate, Anna talked freely with the nurse, but Dirk

found it hard to concentrate. He occasionally nodded to make it seem like he was listening. It was hard to figure out Fleischer. Both of his dreams had warned him not to tell Fleischer about Papa. *Hadn't they?* But the colonel already knew about Papa. And Fleischer had helped them.

"Do you have any chocolate?" Anna asked the nurse. "I *love* chocolate."

"Sorry," the nurse answered with a smile. "There's no chocolate on the menu."

Dirk continued eating without paying much attention to the conversation. In his second dream, Fleischer had bragged about the eagle on his uniform. But in real life, Fleischer's pin was different. The eagle's wings he wore went straight across, not turned up like the ones in the dream. Dirk shook his head. What if the dream wasn't a warning about Fleischer? He and Anna were safe now, weren't they? What could happen to them now? Was there someone else Dirk had to watch out for?

As the sun rose, a sergeant approached the children. He was almost two meters tall, about the same height as Papa. But he had short brown hair and was much more muscular than Papa.

"Hello," the man said with a smile. "I am Sergeant Samuel Michaels. I understand you want to go to your grandparents' house."

"Your voice is really deep," Anna said.

Michaels smiled again.

After Dirk answered the sergeant's questions and gave his grandparents' address, he had a question for the sergeant.

"Sir," Dirk asked, "do you have any information about where my father and my older sister are? My papa's name is Hans Ingelse, and my sister's name is Els."

Sergeant Michaels shook his head. "I'm sorry, I don't. You could ask the Dutch authorities."

He ordered a soldier to take Dirk and Anna to a large tent filled with cots. Exhausted by the strain of their trip to the American base, they quickly fell asleep and didn't wake until noon. A soldier led them to the mess tent for another meal. Then Sergeant Michaels and two of his soldiers stood ready to walk them to Oma and Opa's house, which was only a few blocks away.

As soon as they were off the American base, Dutch flags hung everywhere—not just on government buildings and flagpoles, but also draped on the sides of businesses and private homes. And it wasn't a holiday, like Queen's Day. Years of pent-up patriotism had burst forth after the city's liberation. It was so good to see so many flags.

"We're going to see Oma and Opa!" Anna said. She bounced as they walked.

Sergeant Michaels motioned Dirk to come closer. "Have you heard from your grandparents in the last few months?" he said softly.

"No, why?" Dirk slowed his pace.

The other soldiers stayed with Anna. In her exuberance to see Oma and Opa, she moved well ahead of Sergeant Michaels and Dirk.

"How much do you know about what's happened here in Nijmegen?" the sergeant asked.

"I guess not anything really. Why?" Dirk's throat tightened.

"I don't know how to tell you this."

Dirk's heart beat so hard he was surprised the sergeant couldn't hear it.

"In the battle to liberate Nijmegen a lot of buildings were damaged. Especially in this part of town."

Dirk stopped walking. "Did something happen to my grandparents' house?"

"I hope not, but we'll see in a few minutes when we get there."

Dirk forced himself to start walking again. At this point they turned a corner, and Dirk's jaw dropped. A girls' school was badly damaged from bombing. On both sides of the street, many homes were damaged, and some were destroyed. A few homes were missing portions, like a roof or outside wall, but many had been completely smashed. No one in those homes could have survived those direct hits. What if—?

"Dirk!" Anna broke into his thoughts. "Aren't you excited?" Without waiting for a response, she continued, "Can we play hide-and-go-seek? I always go in one bedroom and sneak through the closet that connects to the other bedroom, and you never find me."

Dirk didn't answer. He couldn't. His slow gait and silence contrasted with Anna's lively steps and chatter.

He tried but failed at forcing a smile.

"Do you think they'll be home?" she asked.

"Yes," he managed to get out. *If their house hasn't been crushed.* "It's Sunday afternoon, and they're probably taking a nap." But he turned his face away, and when his right hand twitched, he withdrew it into his jacket sleeve. If their house was destroyed, even taking shelter in the basement wouldn't have saved Oma and Opa. And then who would take care of Dirk and Anna? Who would help them find Papa? As they approached the last corner, his steps slowed even more, and his gaze fell to the pavement immediately in front of him.

"There it is!" Anna shouted. She burst into a run. Dirk hesitated and then looked up. The windows and walls were intact, and a rope hung from the roof, down to the ground. As Anna continued running, Dirk stood stock still, staring at the house. Tears formed in his eyes. *Maybe things are finally turning our way.* Hope blossomed in his heart like a field of tulips in April.

CHAPTER TWENTY

THE SERGEANT CLIMBED the porch steps and knocked on the door. Anna bounced up and down, and Dirk tried to catch a glimpse of Oma or Opa through the windows in the front door. "Who is it?" a man's voice said from inside.

"I am Sergeant Samuel Michaels of the United States Army. I've brought your two grandchildren." The door opened a crack.

"It's us!" Anna squealed.

A portion of Opa's face appeared through the small window in the front door. A moment later the door flew open. Opa rushed onto the porch and hugged Dirk and Anna.

"What's all the commotion?" Oma called from inside the house. When she reached the door, her eyes grew wide. She dashed across the threshold and took Dirk and Anna in her embrace.

"I can't believe you're here!" she spluttered. "It's so good to see you!" The four Ingelses stood there for a minute, hugging and smiling, tears flowing freely.

"Thank you so much for bringing our grandchildren," Opa said. He pumped Sergeant Michaels's hand up and down. "I can't thank all of you enough." He gave each of the soldiers a hearty handshake.

"We're glad to serve," the sergeant replied, smiling. "But now we have to go back to our base."

Opa shook each of the soldiers' hands again, and Oma hugged them. The soldiers said goodbye to Dirk and Anna and left.

"Come in, come in," Opa said, and the four of them settled in the living room. Anna climbed onto Oma's lap, and Dirk and Opa sat across from them.

"It's wonderful to see you, but how did you get here?" Oma asked. "And why isn't Els with you?"

"It was terrible, Oma. The Gestapo captured her," Dirk said.

"What?! Why?"

"They took her as a way of getting to Papa. And one of our neighbors said the Gestapo would come after Anna and me next, so we had to leave right away."

Oma stroked Anna's hair. "You poor dears. When did you leave home?"

"On November 11," Dirk said.

"The 11th! Today's the 26th! What took you so long? Are you all right?" Opa asked.

"The moffen captured us in Doorwerth and forced us to work in a factory. Then we escaped and hid in a farmhouse, but we weren't really safe there, either," Dirk said.

Opa shook his head. "How did you get to Nijmegen?"

"Oh. That's a long story. But we got a ride to the American base here, and Sergeant Michaels and his soldiers brought us to the house."

"I want to hear more about it," Oma said. "But first, stand back and let me have a good look at you." She cringed. "You're both so thin."

"We didn't have much to eat at the gun factory," Dirk said.

"Let's get you some food, then. Now that the moffen are gone from our part of the Netherlands, we can get you something to eat," Oma said, starting toward the kitchen. "But we still don't have as much food as—"

"Oh, let's not worry the children about that just yet," Opa said.

"We just ate at the army base," Dirk told his grandparents, patting his stomach. "But it feels so good to see you and to be safe."

"You left out the good parts of the story, Dirk. Let *me* tell it," Anna said with a hint of a scowl.

"All right."

"Well, first we had to leave the house, and Dirk forgot to bring my doll," she said.

He shook his head.

"We went to Tante Cora's, but some soldiers grabbed us, and we had to work really hard, and my hands got blisters."

"Oh no," Oma said, wincing.

"But it was all right 'cause I helped Dirk be brave."

Dirk's eyebrows shot up.

"Then bombers came, and I told Dirk to run."

"Wait," he said. "That's not how—"

"You said I could tell it," Anna said.

Dirk shrugged his shoulders. *This might be interesting.*

"The bombs fell, and they went *BOOM, BOOM*," Anna said as she made exploding motions with her hands. "So we ran away. Then we walked and walked until a German truck came down the road, and we hid in the weeds. Dirk didn't know what to do, so I helped him hide."

Is Opa smiling?

"Then we walked more until I found a farm where we could hide. When we got to the barn, Dirk went to the house to ask for help."

I finally get credit for something.

"But I had the really hard part," she continued, "'cause I had to stay in the barn all by myself. And the farmer and his wife took us in. Their names are Mr. and Mrs. ten Haken. Colonel Fleischer was there too. He was a German officer, but he wasn't working for the Nazis anymore."

Anna took a deep breath and then took off again, like a refueled fighter plane.

"I kept telling Dirk that Colonel Fleischer was nice, but Dirk wouldn't listen to me. Then he finally believed me and asked Colonel Fleischer to drive us to the American soldiers. But first some German soldiers shot at us—"

"What?" Oma exclaimed. Her hands flew up to her cheeks.

"But I knew they wouldn't get us," Anna continued with a wave of her hand, "'cause I prayed, but Dirk isn't a good driver, and he drove right into a wall."

Opa's eyebrows flew up. "Dirk was driving?"

"Uh-huh. But we got through it," Anna continued, "and

then the soldiers talked to us and took Colonel Fleischer away, and I miss him 'cause he gave me chocolate, and now I won't get any more from him. But that's what war is like. Sometimes it's hard." She nodded at them with a straight face.

"That's quite a story, Anna, and it sounds to me like you were very brave," Opa said with a twinkle in his eye.

"Yeah, I pretty much was, but I didn't do it all by myself. Dirk helped a little too," Anna conceded.

"Whah, ha, ha!" Laughter erupted from deep inside Dirk. "Oh, Anna!" Sitting in the chair, he bent forward, his face contorted and his abdomen contracted in happy convulsions. Oma and Opa joined in the merriment.

"What's so funny?" Anna asked.

"Oh," Dirk said, as he gasped for air. "It feels so good to laugh again!" Then he succumbed to another round of laughter. After another thirty seconds of belly laughing, he subsided into a broad smile.

"Yes, it feels good to laugh, and it feels even better to have you here," Opa said. After a brief silence, he checked his watch and said, "Oh! I have to go to a meeting about helping people whose homes got damaged by the war."

For the next hour, Anna and Dirk told Oma about more of their adventures. During a pause in the conversation, Anna yawned.

"Somebody needs a nap," Oma said as she patted Anna on the head.

"But I'm not tired," she objected as she yawned again.

"Follow me. You can sleep in our bedroom."

Anna pouted. "But I always sleep upstairs."

"You can sleep there tonight, but it's too cold now. We closed the heat register because we haven't been using that room."

A few minutes later, Oma returned to the living room after settling Anna in for her nap.

Dirk walked to a window and pointed outside. "Why do you have a rope hanging from your roof?"

"It's to get a large dresser up to the second floor tomorrow," Oma said. "It will be easier to do it with the rope and a pulley than to take it up the narrow stairway."

Dirk nodded.

"I'm going to visit a friend who lives a few blocks away," she told Dirk. "Her children are the same ages as you and Anna. I'll ask them for spare clothes so you won't have to wear these clothes that are hanging off you. And with the weather so cold, you need jackets that fit you too. The ones you got from the soldiers are too big. I won't be gone long." She left a few minutes later.

With the house quiet, Dirk had time to think. It felt good not having to worry about protecting Anna. *But where are Papa and Els?*

CHAPTER TWENTY-ONE

LUFTWAFFE BASE
ROTTERDAM
NOVEMBER 26

As ELS WALKED into the office, instead of looking at the German officer who worked at his wood desk, she kept her steely stare half a meter above his head. *Heart of stone.* No one had found the little pebble she'd hid in her mouth, and now it lay tucked into a corner of her new cell.

A modest fire burned in a fireplace two meters to Els's left. A chair sat near it. "Please take a seat," the officer said. He moved his chair in front of her and sat as well. She pushed her chair back until it hit the wall behind her.

The officer's hat, which sat on his desk, bore the insignia of an eagle clutching a Nazi swastika in its talons, the way an eagle might grasp a fish. *Or the way the Nazis seized the Netherlands.* She looked the officer over. He appeared to be in his mid-forties with light brown hair. He wore several medals on his uniform.

The officer turned back toward the desk and poured coffee from a silver pot into two cups. "I am Captain Schmidt." He held a cup of coffee out to her. "Would you like cream or sugar?"

She hesitated. *Why is he being nice?*

"Sugar," she replied in a flat tone of voice.

He passed the coffee to her. She wrapped both hands around the cup, and the warmth seeped into her chilly hands. For a moment she relaxed as she took a sip.

"Please make yourself comfortable," he continued in a friendly tone. "You are no longer in the custody of the Gestapo. Our methods are very different from theirs. I will ask you questions, but I will treat you with respect, because that is how the Luftwaffe operates."

Els's mind flashed back to Captain Adler from the Gestapo, who had seemed nice at first too, and even offered her a glass of water before he slapped her face and knocked the drink away from her. She leaned forward and looked Captain Schmidt in the eye. "You're going to try to get information out of me. But the Gestapo couldn't, and you won't either." She pointed to a big bruise on her arm. "A man they call the Iron Fist said he always got people to talk. I didn't."

"I do not need to press you for secrets," Schmidt said. "I already know a great deal about you and your family, so I just need you to confirm a few basic facts so I can satisfy my superiors."

Els scoffed. "You don't fool me," she said. "You're only paying me with monkey coins."

"Excuse me?" Schmidt asked.

"It's a saying we Dutch have which means that someone is trying to deceive us with nice words."

"What an interesting expression. But I assure you that what I have told you is quite true."

Els set her coffee down unfinished. She crossed her arms and glared at Schmidt.

"You grew up on a farm outside Oosterbeek, near Arnhem, where you have one cow. You used to have a dog named Mees. Last summer you raised potatoes and sugar beets."

How does he know so much?

"I'm not going to tell you anything about my family," she said.

"I have news that will interest you." He paused. "Your brother and sister are no longer at your farm. I hope they are safe."

Els shifted in her chair.

"Your mother passed away two months ago. I extend my sympathy to you," Schmidt said softly. "And your father is well known to us. He is a leader in the Dutch Resistance, and he left your farm three months ago."

"He's too clever for you to ever catch him," she said.

"He puts sugar cubes in the gas tanks of our trucks to ruin the engines, and he teaches others how to sabotage train tracks."

Els's eyes widened briefly before she overrode her reaction.

"He mixed lime and water in a watering can and poured it on the pavement in front of a Gestapo headquarters. When he finished pouring, the cobblestones looked merely wet. But when they dried, the white lime showed a large *V*, a symbol of the Resistance." He paused. "You must be very proud of him."

"I love my father," Els replied. "But I don't know anything about these things."

"Of course not," Schmidt said. "He would never endanger your safety by telling you."

Els folded her arms and stared at the fireplace.

"I know a great deal about you as well. Your favorite flower is the daffodil, and your best friend's name is Janna." Els's jaw dropped a centimeter, though she managed to keep her lips closed. She quickly clenched her teeth again.

"Oh, where are my manners?" Schmidt said. "You must be hungry. I'll order your favorite snack." He stood. "Guard!" he called. "Bring us some stroopwafels."

"Giving me food won't make me talk," Els said.

Schmidt looked at her with an unchanged expression.

He picked up the silver pot and refilled Els's cup. "I told you I would treat you with respect, because that is how the Luftwaffe operates." The guard returned with a plate of stroopwafels and handed it to Schmidt. The captain held the plate out to Els first. She hesitated, then lifted a thin wafer treat from the plate and placed the cookie atop her mug. The warmth from the coffee began to melt the layer of caramel syrup inside the stroopwafel.

Schmidt took a bite from his own stroopwafel, sipped his coffee, and then set the cup down. "As I said before, I know a great deal about you. You are an impressive young woman."

Els visualized the small stone in the corner of her cell as

she stared at him with a blank expression. "Flattery won't work either," she said.

"At social gatherings," he continued, "you stole identity cards which your father used to help American pilots make it back to England after their planes were shot down. You dyed the hair of Jewish women blonde to help them escape." He sipped his coffee again.

The stroopwafel's warm now. She lifted the Dutch treat off her mug and took a bite. She closed her eyes and relished the sweet, sticky insides of the thin cookie.

"You delivered messages for the Resistance, but you had an excuse for every trip. You also carried milk or eggs in case someone asked why you were going there."

He's guessing. Don't show any emotion.

"You carried false identity papers, letters, and messages. What were those messages about?"

Els turned her head to the right and fixed her gaze on the open door.

"Your father was involved with the failed Operation Market Garden. When he helped evacuate paratroopers, did you take messages regarding their whereabouts?"

She crossed her arms and stared into his eyes without blinking.

"Did you ever deliver money?"

She looked around his office as if she were sitting alone. She finished the last of her stroopwafel and coffee.

"The Gestapo is searching aggressively for your father, and when they find him, it will not go well for him," Schmidt said.

Els glared at him.

"He risks his life for Jews, but we capture them anyway a few weeks later."

"You're lying!"

"Am I? I received a report from Berlin which says more Jews have been captured in the Netherlands than in any other European country. Your father's plan isn't working, and he will die for nothing."

Els stuck out her chin. "The Gestapo will never catch Papa."

"Do you really think that dozens of people will choose your father's safety over their own families having enough food to eat? It only takes one person to tell on him." He tapped his pen on the desk. "But," Schmidt said, his face brightening, "if you help us find him, he will remain in Luftwaffe custody. We will not hand him over to the Gestapo. When the war ends, he will still be alive."

Els smacked her hand on the armrest of her chair. "How stupid do you think I am? You don't care about protecting my father. It's your last desperate ploy to capture a man who is smarter than all of you. And if he is such a failure, why are you moving heaven and earth to find him?" She stabbed a finger toward Schmidt. "And now you have the gall to ask his own daughter to betray him!"

Schmidt sat in silence for a long while. "I can see that you won't talk, but I had to try." He shrugged, then handed her a document and a pen. "I just need you to look at this form," he said. "Confirm your name and age, and that you are from Oosterbeek." He smiled. "My interrogation will then be complete, and I can submit my paperwork."

Els frowned as she studied the form. *I guess I can sign this. He already knows it.* She signed her name and returned the pen and paper to Schmidt.

He put her signed form in a file folder. "Thank you, Els. Is there anything else you would like to say?"

"Yes," she replied. "After the Great War ended in 1918, the Dutch people fed and clothed orphans from Germany." She stood and pointed a finger at Schmidt. "They're grown now, and they are the generation who repays us for saving their lives by starving us!" She sat back down with such force that the chair banged against the wall behind her.

"I have recorded your comments, Els. Guard! Bring lunch for two to my office."

"Yes, sir!"

"The food will be here soon," Schmidt said. "Please relax while I finish some work."

Ten minutes later, the guard returned with two dishes of beef and potato soup. As he served the steaming bowls to Els and the captain, Schmidt remarked, "I don't mind admitting that I am looking forward to some polite conversation after a morning of paperwork."

Els's mouth watered. *It's the first hot food I've had since the Gestapo arrested me.*

Schmidt picked up his spoon. "I've always admired the Dutch. The Dutch masters are some of the greatest painters of all time. Before the war, I really enjoyed my visit to the Rijksmuseum." He swallowed a spoonful of soup. "Do you enjoy art?"

She nodded with her mouth full.

"I have children, and they aren't always interested in the things I would like them to be interested in." He chuckled. "My admiration for the Dutch reminds me of a question. Your people are wonderful ice skaters. Is it hard to learn?"

Before she could answer, the guard returned with two plates of food. He waited as they finished their soup, then handed a plate of food to each of them, along with a fork and knife. Els stared. *I can't believe I get this much food! The sauerbraten smells so good.*

"It's easier for children to learn to skate," she answered as she stabbed her fork into the hot German pot roast. The aroma filled her nostrils. "Mama was French, and she tried to learn as an adult." She smiled. "But she didn't do very well. My little sister, Anna, who was only four years old at the time, did circles, while Mama struggled to avoid falling."

Schmidt returned her smile. "Please enlighten me about something else," he said. "Why do so many Dutch people ride bicycles? I have never seen anything like it. Was it that way before the war?"

Els said nothing for a few moments while she chewed a mouthful of food. "Yes, it was that way before the war. I don't know why, but I think it's always been that way."

"It's too bad many of you will have to quit riding since you can't get rubber for your Resistance couriers' bicycles."

Els's nostrils flared. "You're wrong!" She set her fork down with a loud clank. "We'll never quit riding. Some of us make wheels out of wood, and others take flat tires and fasten the rubber to the wheel. But we still ride, and we always will.

Riding our bikes reminds us that we're still Dutch, no matter what your soldiers do to us."

"Oh, the fire has gone down," Schmidt said. He walked to the fireplace, added two logs, and returned to his seat.

For the remainder of the meal, the conversation meandered over a variety of topics, including the cold weather, favorite pieces of music, and Els's career plans.

"You have been a most pleasant conversation partner," Schmidt said after they finished eating. "Guard! Take Els back to her cell."

He stood and extended his hand toward Els. She kept her hands by her side.

"I enjoyed our conversation even though I couldn't pry anything out of you."

"I told you I wouldn't tell you anything," Els said. The guard escorted her back to her cell.

● ● ●

Schmidt walked to his desk, opened a file, smiled, and wrote, "Break the Dutch spirit by taking away their bicycles. Depriving them of rubber is not enough. The bicycles must be eliminated altogether."

CHAPTER TWENTY-TWO

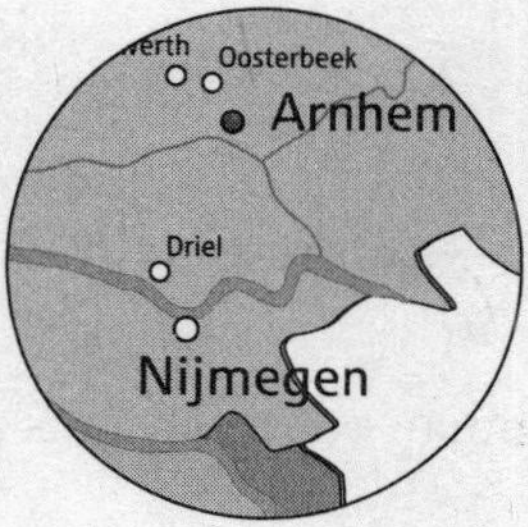
Oosterbeek
Arnhem
Driel
Nijmegen

OMA AND OPA'S HOME
NIJMEGEN

With the house quiet, Dirk looked around for something to do. A book of Dutch fairy tales lay on the coffee table in the living room. He picked it up and read "The Curly-Tailed Lion" and "The Farm That Ran Away and Came Back."

Someone knocked on the front door. Dirk walked to it and peered through the window. A woman of perhaps sixty years of age stood on the porch. Dirk didn't recognize her but opened the door. Maybe this was one of Oma's friends. He'd just find out what the woman wanted and tell Oma when she returned. "Hello," he said with a polite smile.

"Good morning. My name is Hendrika Vandermolen," she began in a soft voice. "I work for the Dutch Defense Department." She had a dark brown hat, which covered most of her hair, and a matching jacket with a pin on it. "So many children have been uprooted or lost their parents in the war, and we want to be sure all our wonderful Dutch children are cared for."

She moved forward and extended her hand toward Dirk.

He took a step back.

"Are your parents living?"

Dirk froze. Mama had warned him not to say who he was or who Papa was.

"Did you hear what I asked you?" she asked with a tinge of impatience.

He stared at the silver pin on the woman's coat, and his eyes grew wide.

"Young man, I'm talking to you." Her voice was a bit louder this time.

She's wearing an eagle pin, with the wings turned up at the end just like in the dream when Fleischer attacked me!

"I asked you a simple question. Are your parents living?" the woman asked.

His blood ran cold.

"Where are your parents?" she was nearly shouting now.

"Uh, why do you ask?" Dirk managed to get out. Should he tell her he was staying with his grandparents? Something told him not to reveal that.

Vandermolen pushed her way into the house, and immediately behind her came a broad-shouldered man two meters tall. He bumped Dirk out of the way and said to the woman, "Never mind. I'll have a look and find out."

"What do you want?" Dirk asked the woman. His right hand shook.

"We only want to keep you safe," she cooed. "We're authorized to take you to a safe place where you will be cared for. Parents will be notified to search for their children at the safe houses. We have a truck waiting."

That big ape was looking around, and Dirk couldn't let him find Anna. He looked past the woman through the open door. No neighbors were outside for him to cry out to for help. What could he do? He bit his lip, turned away from the woman, and closed his eyes for a moment.

Then he turned back to the woman, smiled, and said, "Thank you for your kind offer. I need to go upstairs first."

She nodded. He had to act calm and climb the stairs slowly, but it was difficult with his heart jackhammering. Her large companion turned toward the back hallway where Anna slept. Dirk hadn't reached the top of the stairs, but he couldn't wait any longer. *Sometimes you have to take a chance because it's the only chance you have.*

"Hey!" Dirk shouted and glared at the man, anger fueling his courage. Dirk made a fist and shook it at him. "You stupid oaf! If you're such a tough guy, come and get me!" *Sorry, Mama, but I have to lead him away from Anna.*

Dirk darted inside a second-floor bedroom, closed the door, and locked it. Footsteps pounded up the steps, and he hurriedly shoved a heavy dresser up against the door. A moment later, the doorknob rattled.

"What's the matter?" Dirk sneered. "Forgot your keys? It's too bad you're too weak to break the door open."

Dirk flew to the window on the other side of the room. He pushed the curtains aside and jerked the window halfway open. Chilly air washed over him. Then he darted to the closet.

The bedroom door trembled under the force of repeated blows.

"I hope you won't hurt yourself against the big, strong door since your muscles are so puny!" Dirk hollered. But what if bashing the door woke Anna, and she came out of her room? He swallowed hard. The only thing he could do was continue the plan and hope for the best.

Inside the closet, he pulled the door shut behind him. In utter darkness, he felt his way through the clothing. Then, like Anna had done a hundred times before during hide-and-go-seek, he crawled to the closet of the adjoining room. He clawed through another set of clothes, stepped into the next bedroom, and closed the closet door behind him. He slid a dresser in front of the closet door.

He raced to the window in that bedroom and pushed up. It didn't budge. In the meantime, it sounded like the brute was assaulting the door in the other room with his fists and feet. That was quickly followed by a loud crashing sound. *Didn't take him long to destroy the door.* Dirk pushed harder on the window. He had to get it open, or he'd be trapped by this muscular man he'd antagonized.

"Where are you? You're not so brave now that I broke down the door," a voice bellowed from the other room. The window in the first bedroom creaked. *He thinks I escaped onto the roof. Fooled him!*

But his angry enemy would soon give up on the roof and come after Dirk again. He pushed on his window again until his hands and wrists hurt. It didn't budge. He reached up to the top of the window and pulled down, using his body weight. Then he bent his legs to push up with his arms and his legs. "Unnhh!" a low-pitched growl rose from his throat, like the rumble of a diesel engine revving for power. He pushed on the window as if his life depended on it. Because it did. The joints in his arms and wrists screamed for him to stop, and his face grew red from the exertion. Finally something popped in the window, and it slid open. As his chest heaved, the closet door in the other bedroom opened and heavy footsteps thudded closer in the closet.

"Don't cry for your mommy because you're scared of the dark closet," Dirk shouted over his shoulder. Then he put one leg through the open window. As he straddled the base of the window frame, he grabbed the rope hanging from the roof. Hand over hand, he lowered himself.

When he reached the ground, he sprinted toward the American military base. If only he had a bicycle. After he ran two blocks, his legs grew heavy, his lungs burned, and the brisk wind stung his cheeks and ears. He had to keep going a little farther. *For Anna.* When he reached the base, he spotted a familiar face at the gate.

"Sergeant Michaels! Help!" he shouted through gasps for air.

Michaels stood up and stepped forward. "Dirk! What's the matter?"

"A man and a woman barged into our house." He took a quick breath. "They're going to kidnap Anna!"

"Follow me," Michaels said. He grabbed a rifle and shouted an order to the two soldiers he had taken with him before. The three soldiers and Dirk ran to a nearby jeep, and they roared off toward the house. *Please let us make it back in time.*

"Hurry!" Dirk urged.

"I'll go to the front door," Michaels shouted to his men above the noise of the accelerating jeep. "You enter from the back."

The vehicle skidded to a stop in front of the house. Michaels vaulted onto the front porch while the other soldiers sprinted to the back door.

The sergeant grabbed the doorknob on the front door, but it was locked.

"You have a key?" the sergeant asked Dirk.

"No."

"I'll use my master key," Michaels said. He swung his rifle at the door and broke open one of its small windows with the rifle butt. After the window shattered, he reached inside, unlocked the door, and burst into the house. Dirk followed him in.

The woman with the eagle pin sat by a desk in the living room, rummaging through the drawers.

"United States Army!" Michaels announced. "Lie facedown on the floor."

She obeyed his order.

Dirk looked around wildly for her accomplice. *What if that man already found Anna?*

Anna walked into the living room, rubbing her eyes.

"What was that noise?" she asked. She was about three meters from the woman.

"Stay where you are, Anna," Dirk said.

The woman, still lying on the floor, slid her right leg toward Anna.

"Stop moving," Michaels ordered. "That little girl and her brother are under the protection of the United States Army, and they are my friends." The other soldiers entered the room after they had come in through the back door.

The woman raised her eyebrows and asked, "You wouldn't shoot a lady, would you?"

"A woman who barges into a house and threatens children is not a lady!"

"Dirk, who is that woman?" Anna asked.

He rushed to Anna's side. "It's okay now. The soldiers won't let her hurt us," he said. He draped an arm over her shoulder.

Motioning to one soldier, the sergeant said, "Keep an eye on this woman."

An upstairs bedroom door opened, and the woman's large accomplice appeared at the top of the stairs. He glared at Dirk and made a crushing motion with both hands. "You made a big mistake in coming back."

He stopped talking when his eyes met Sergeant Michaels's gaze.

"Put your hands up," Michaels said. "Come down here and lie facedown next to your friend." He pointed his rifle at the burly man.

"Your toy gun doesn't scare me," the man sneered as he headed down the steps. "I'm going to break you in half with my bare hands."

Michaels burst out laughing. "I grew up in Chicago, and

I've faced bigger and meaner people than you. Do as I say, or my friend here," he tapped his rifle, "will do the talking for me."

The other man reached the bottom of the stairs and glared at Michaels in a silent standoff. Finally, the man lay facedown.

Michaels motioned to another soldier.

"Keep an eye on him," he said, nodding toward the man on the floor. Michaels dashed outside, and Dirk watched through the open front door as the sergeant approached a delivery truck. Michaels looked in the back of the truck, walked to the front, and motioned the driver to get out with his hands up. Finally there was an adult to take charge and stop the Nazis instead of it always being up to Dirk to protect Anna.

Michaels motioned for the driver to walk in front of him, enter the house, and lie facedown on the floor, next to the older woman and the burly man.

"Where are your grandparents?" Michaels asked Dirk.

"Opa's at a meeting. Oma's at a friend's house. She'll be back soon," Dirk said.

Michaels used the telephone to call the American base. When he finished, he told Dirk, "Military police will take these suspects into custody. My men and I will stay here until they're gone and your grandmother comes back. There are children in the back of that truck. I'm going out to tell them what's happening. Then I'll stand guard on the porch until the military police arrive to take care of these troublemakers and bring the children to safety."

CHAPTER TWENTY-THREE

A FEW MINUTES LATER, Oma arrived. She was horrified to hear what had happened but relieved at how it had turned out. She thanked the soldiers and then gave Dirk and Anna the clothing she had borrowed from her friend. "Go put these clothes on and get out of the ones they gave you at the farm. You'll feel much better in clothes your size," she said.

Anna clung to Dirk. "We're safe now. You don't have to worry," he said. But he kept looking out the front windows at the street. Several times he asked Oma how soon Opa would be home. All their hardships were supposed to be over once they arrived at Oma and Opa's house. And then this had happened.

Shortly after Dirk and Anna changed their clothes, the military police arrived. They escorted the suspects out of the house and drove the children who had been waiting in the truck to the American base.

After they left, Dirk asked, "Why did those people want to kidnap us, Oma?"

"They probably wanted to hold you for ransom."

"Do you think they were collaborators?" Dirk asked.

"What?" Anna asked.

"Some Dutch people help the Nazis," Dirk told her. "They're tattletales who tell the Germans which Dutch people are fighting the Germans and helping Jews."

"Why do they do that?" Anna asked angrily.

"The Germans give these people money or food," Sergeant Michaels said. "But I don't know if these people were collaborators," he added.

"I hate the Nazis!" exclaimed Anna.

"If they weren't collaborators, then why did they want to kidnap us?" Dirk asked.

"Our country is still getting on its feet," Oma said. "And some people may try to take advantage of the temporary disorder. But we're thankful the soldiers kept you safe." She hugged each of the soldiers.

"Just doing our jobs," Sergeant Michaels said, and then he and his soldiers left.

When Opa returned, he listened intently to what had happened.

"You lured the man into chasing you, to protect Anna. How did you think of that?" Opa asked Dirk.

Dirk smiled. "Anna gave me the idea."

She scrunched up her nose and looked at him.

"At the ten Hakens' house, we hid in a barn until we could leave with Colonel Fleischer. Anna got upset when a cat chased an injured bird. But the bird was only pretending she was hurt in order to lure the cat away from her baby birds in the nest. So I realized that was how I had to get that man away from Anna."

"That was quick thinking, Dirk," Opa said.

It felt so good to be with Oma and Opa. Unlike the Nazis, when Oma and Opa said something nice, they meant it. They weren't just paying him with monkey coins.

Opa promptly went to work to replace the broken window in the front door. When he finished, he locked the door.

At dinner, Oma lifted the lid off the cooking pot. Steam rose, and Dirk inhaled deeply.

"Stamppot!" he cried. "Ohhh!"

The aroma of sausage, potatoes, and onions filled the kitchen. After dinner, the four family members talked and played games.

At bedtime, Oma said, "Anna, you may sleep upstairs because I opened the heat register this afternoon. Get ready for bed, and I'll come up to tuck you in."

Anna nodded, then thrust her hand, palm up, in front of Dirk's face.

"I want my ribbon from Papa. You promised."

He pulled it out of his pocket and gave it to her. She clasped it with both hands and held it against her right cheek. "Papa," she sighed as she climbed the stairs.

Once she was out of earshot, Dirk asked his grandparents, "Do you think Papa and Els are all right?"

"I pray for them every day, and I hope for the best," Opa replied.

"Papa and Els used to say, 'Keep your hopes up and your prayers strong,'" Dirk said.

Opa nodded. "That's good advice for these challenging times. I heard on the radio that the Allies are making progress, but things are getting a lot worse in the parts of the Netherlands still controlled by the Germans, like Rotterdam and Amsterdam."

"Oh no," Oma said, putting her hand on her forehead.

"The Germans cut off food and coal supplies, so people have been starving and freezing. They're burning furniture, cupboards, and every other step on their wood stairs."

"It was like that at Tante Cora's house too," Dirk said. He hoped Tante Cora was all right and not worrying about them too much.

"Those poor people," Oma said.

Dirk shook his head. "I just hope Papa and Els aren't there."

● ● ●

DE NESSE STREET

ROTTERDAM

NOVEMBER 27

A doctor stepped inside a modest white house with bright blue shutters on De Nesse Street in Rotterdam.

"How is she?" he asked as he handed his coat to a middle-aged woman. She was about one and a half meters tall and wore her fading blonde hair in a ponytail.

"She's in a lot of pain," the woman said with a grimace. "She's lucky to be alive, considering what happened."

"Oh?"

"Yesterday the Allies accidentally bombed a residential

neighborhood and crushed a former monastery which the Luftwaffe was using as a prison. All the guards died, but she survived because her holding cell was heavily reinforced."

"How did she get here?" the doctor asked.

"Dutch Resistance workers dug her out of the rubble and brought her here."

"May I see her now?" He raised his eyebrows. "What is her name?"

"We didn't exchange names. It's safer that way, in case one of us gets captured."

"Oh. Of course."

"Follow me." The woman led him to a bedroom at the end of the hall. "I've been told the Germans are looking for her."

"They must have searched the bombed prison, and when they didn't find her body—"

"They realized she escaped," the woman finished. "She has to leave Rotterdam, but we don't know if she's healthy enough to travel."

The doctor stepped into the room, set his medical bag on the floor, and looked at the young woman on the bed in front of him. "May I examine you?"

"Yes." She winced from the effort of sitting up.

"I see bruises on your face. Are there others?"

"A few, but the biggest problem is my head. I have terrible headaches, and I, uh . . . have a hard time . . . concentrating and . . . remembering new things."

"Did these symptoms start after the bombing?"

She nodded and clutched her forehead.

For several minutes, he asked questions and gave her a

medical exam. As he put his stethoscope away, he looked at the older woman and said, "She has a concussion. It's not severe, but she needs rest."

"Can she use a bicycle? She's got to get out of here."

"No. She needs rest and food. Have a doctor check her again in a week." He closed his medical bag.

"How can she get enough to eat when everyone in Rotterdam is hungry?" the older woman asked. "We're down to eating dog food, and it's almost gone."

"That's one more reason to hope the war will end soon," the doctor said.

"Thank you, sir. Keep your hopes up and your prayers strong," the younger woman said with effort.

"I agree." He turned to the older woman and said, "I can find my way out."

The next morning the older woman bit her lip. "It's too bad you can't travel yet. The Germans could show up any day now looking for you."

"I know. And I have to get to, uh . . . Nijmegen, to my oma and opa's house. Maybe they'll know . . . if my brother and sister made it to our aunt's house."

"But we can't sneak you out of here. Collaborators are watching the house." The older woman wrung her hands. "We have to do something, but what?"

CHAPTER TWENTY-FOUR

OMA AND OPA'S HOUSE
NIJMEGEN

I_N THE DAYS THAT FOLLOWED_, Dirk and Anna settled into a routine of chores mixed with play. Anna giggled each time her grandparents or Dirk didn't find her in hide-and-go-seek.

The next Saturday, the morning sun streamed through the upstairs window and collected on the floor in puddles of light in Dirk's bedroom. Lazy specks of dust swirled slowly in the sunshine. He lay in bed, a lump under a cozy pile of blankets.

Hours later, Opa took the stairs to Dirk's bedroom. *Knock, knock, knock.* Dirk didn't stir.

"Good morning, sleepyhead," Opa said as he opened the door. Dirk's eyelids fluttered, Opa's words piercing his consciousness like a Dutch lighthouse beacon that slices the North Atlantic fog. A few minutes later, Dirk and Anna came downstairs. After breakfast they lounged in their pajamas and read books for the rest of the morning.

"How soon do you think we'll hear about Papa and Els?" Dirk asked at lunch.

"I don't know," Opa said, "but as soon as we hear anything, we'll let you know. But we're all going to a town meeting at St. Stephen's Church in a couple of hours."

"What's the meeting for?" Dirk asked.

"Now that the Germans are gone," Oma said, "the American military has set up a temporary government. They'll tell us about the plans for getting more food to Nijmegen."

"Wait," Dirk said. "This part of the Netherlands is liberated, and you're still not getting enough food?"

"We have a lot more food than we used to, but not as much as we need, because the first priority is getting food and supplies to the military."

Anna wrinkled her nose. "Why is the meeting in a church?"

"It's the only building still intact that's large enough for the community to meet," Opa said.

"Can we ask them about Papa and Els?" Dirk asked.

Anna stopped chewing and looked at her grandparents.

Opa cleared his throat and set his fork down. "Well, yes, of course, we can ask. But I don't know how much information like that the Americans will have. They are putting their energies into finishing the war."

Dirk didn't eat much and sat silent for the rest of the meal.

Oma put her hand on Dirk's shoulder when they'd all finished eating. "We all miss them. But I'm glad you and Anna are here, and we'll hope for the best for your papa and Els."

Thirty minutes later, they all walked across the street to the church. Inside the building, the large wooden doors to the sanctuary were propped open, and sunlight poured in through stained-glass windows.

Because the sanctuary was nearly full, Opa selected a pew near the back. At the start of the meeting a gray-haired minister, who looked to be about eighty years old, stood, and with the use of a cane, he shuffled to the front of the platform. He stroked his gray, bushy beard, adjusted his thick glasses, and leaned on the pulpit for support.

"Good morning," he began. His voice was very low, and he had a strong French accent.

"I am Pierre Henri, the assistant pastor of a church in Lyon, France. I am filling in for your minister while he recovers from surgery. We are pleased to offer our sanctuary for this important meeting. I turn the meeting over to Major Douglas Cox from the United States Army Corps Headquarters."

"Good afternoon," the major began. "It is so good to look out and see families here today. I see fathers, mothers, and their children."

Why did he have to say fathers? For the rest of the meeting, Dirk caught only snatches of the instructions about where to go if people needed food or shelter. Mostly he recalled memories of Papa. "Teach me another wrestling move, Papa!" he had said many times. A favorite memory was the first time he'd pinned his father, and Papa had flashed a big grin. It was shortly before he went away. Dirk reached in his pocket and ran his finger over the stone from Papa.

The next thing Dirk knew, the meeting was over, and people were standing.

Oma and Anna went home, but Dirk and Opa stayed

to talk to the major. After they waited in a long line, Cox motioned them forward to speak to him.

"Hello, Major," Opa said. "We are so grateful that you've liberated our town from the Germans."

"You're welcome," the major said.

Opa fiddled with his hat and lowered his voice as he leaned a bit closer to Major Cox. "We're trying to find our son and granddaughter. Do you have any news of the whereabouts of Hans or Els Ingelse from Oosterbeek?"

"Let me check." The major grabbed a briefcase, propped it on a nearby chair, and pulled a folder out. For about a minute he scrutinized the contents of a file. Dirk looked back and forth between Opa and Major Cox.

"Hmm," Major Cox said. He raised his eyebrows and studied the page in his hand.

Opa took a step toward him, and Dirk took a quick, sharp breath. Could this be the answer to his hopes?

Lines of concentration formed on the major's forehead. He slid his index finger down a column of names.

Dirk's gaze followed that finger, willing it to find Papa's and Els's names. But when his finger reached the bottom of the page, the major grimaced.

"No, unfortunately I don't have any record of those names."

Opa took a small step forward and whispered, "Hans is with the Resistance, and the Gestapo has made capturing him a priority. We have to find him before they do!"

"And the Gestapo captured Els," Dirk added. "Who knows how they're torturing her." He shuddered.

"I'm sorry," Major Cox said. "I am *very* sorry, but I don't have any information. You may inquire again in a few days." A grim-faced Opa and the major shook hands.

When they got back to the house, Dirk turned down Anna's request to play hide-and-go-seek, went straight to his bedroom, and closed the door.

•   •   •

"Any news?" Oma asked her husband.

He shook his head. He looked around until he located Anna in the next room.

"It could mean they don't know," he whispered, "but what I'm more afraid of is that the enemy is looking for Hans really hard, and the Allies know where he is but don't dare tell anyone lest the Nazis find out."

Oma hugged Opa. "If you're right, it makes me wonder what kind of dangerous assignment he's on now."

CHAPTER TWENTY-FIVE

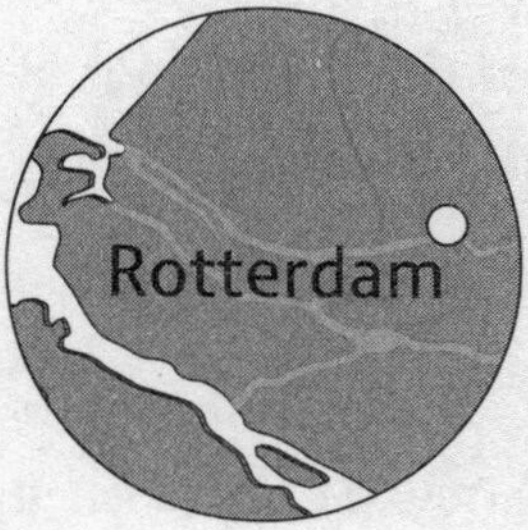
Rotterdam

DE NESSE STREET

ROTTERDAM

DECEMBER 2

THAT SAME SATURDAY AFTERNOON, a small black car pulled up in front of the modest white house with bright blue shutters on De Nesse Street in Rotterdam. A tall man got out of the car and strode toward the house. Inside the home, a middle-aged woman heard the car door shut and peered out the window. When the man approached the house, her pulse raced, she gasped, and she lunged for a button on the wall near the front door. A buzzer sounded in the back of the house. "Not much time," she said under her breath as she ran. She flung open the bedroom door and darted in. A fist pounded on the front door.

"Hurry!" she urged. She waved her arms at the young woman who had slid open a small compartment in the wall. The young woman winced and held her side as she stepped in and closed the door behind her. The older woman yanked the sheets, blankets, and pillow from the bed. She hastily folded them and shoved them into the closet. She grasped the edge of the mattress and, with a grunt, turned it over.

Two hands pummeled the front door like a drummer playing a rapid beat. The woman studied the closed door of the hiding place. "Looks good." She scurried to the front of the house.

"Open up," a deep voice demanded. "I'm a doctor."

"Stay calm. Do what you practiced," she said under her breath, trying to calm her racing heartbeat. As she approached the front door, the knocking repeated. It was so hard it rattled the window in the door.

The woman arrived at the front door and looked out at the visitor. She jostled the doorknob and bumped the lock several times, and then she unlocked the door and opened it.

The man burst in and swept the room with his gaze. "I'm here to see the patient." He was a bit less than two meters tall, and very thin. He wore a long tan coat and a dark brown hat.

"What patient?" the woman asked.

"The one at the end of the hall." He pointed toward the back of the house. "I hope she's feeling better," he added, with a softened tone. "I understand a doctor visited her a week ago today."

"You see how little I have in my house. Do I look like someone who could afford to pay a doctor to make a house call?"

"Please forgive my manners," the man said with a smile. "I forgot to tell you that the doctor who came last time could not come today." He leaned forward. "Someone talked," he said quietly. "The doctor has been captured, and I was told to tell you that Peter Hilbelink sent me."

"I'm so sorry you went to all the trouble of coming here, but I'm afraid it's a waste of your time."

"There *is* a patient here!" His face turned red, and he raised his voice. "She's in that room at the end of the hall." He jabbed his finger toward the back of the house.

"Go ahead, doctor, and see for yourself." He stepped briskly past her and strode down the hall with his thin legs, looking like a two-legged spider. *A spider hunting a fly.*

When they reached the closed door, he burst into the room. In front of him lay an empty bed with a bare mattress. There was nothing else in the room.

"Where is she?" he demanded. "She needs to get out of Rotterdam, but she needs to be seen by a doctor to determine if she's able to travel."

"As you can see," the woman said, motioning with her hand, "the room is empty."

He studied her face, then turned his gaze to survey the room. He scanned it slowly from left to right. He approached the bed and placed both of his hands, palms down, on the center of the bed and pressed lightly. He scowled. Then he pulled a stethoscope out of his bag. He put the two earpieces in his ears and held the round metal piece against the wall. He moved it at one-meter intervals, listening. As he listened on the opposite side of the room from where the fugitive hid, the middle-aged woman coughed a few times.

"Stop making noise," the man said.

"I'm sorry, doctor," she said. "I have a touch of a cold."

She coughed three times in a row. He stepped closer to the wall and listened intently for a minute or so. Finally, he jammed the stethoscope into his medical bag, shot an angry look at the woman, and stormed out of the house.

The woman walked to the front door and watched him drive away. She locked the door and watched the street for five minutes. Her breathing was shallow and rapid, and her heart still raced. "Deep, slow breaths," she told herself. *He would probably love to come back and catch me with my guard down.* After a long final look at the street, she walked back to the bedroom.

"He's gone," she announced. The door to the compartment slid open, and the young woman grimaced as she emerged with difficulty from the cramped quarters. The older woman held out a hand to assist her guest.

"Are you all right?"

The younger woman stood and stretched. "Yes. Just a little stiff."

The older woman nodded.

"He wasn't really a doctor, was he?" the younger woman asked.

"No. He was too pushy, and he felt the mattress with both hands."

"Checking for body heat?"

"Yes," the older woman said. "That's why I flipped the mattress. In case he tried a trick like that."

"My papa taught me that one too," the younger woman said.

"And he put a stethoscope on the wall."

"I heard you cough. You baited him into listening on the opposite side of the room, didn't you?"

"Yes," the older woman said. She looked her visitor in the eye. "The Germans will come back, and next time they'll bring dogs to sniff you out."

"I need to leave today," the younger woman said. "I think I'm strong enough now to ride a bicycle, so I'll go to my oma and opa's house. I've been here a week, and my head feels much clearer."

"Yes, you do seem much better." The older woman tapped her cheek with her index finger. "But when you leave, whoever's watching the house will tell the Nazis." Her shoulders slumped. "I don't know what we should do."

"I do," the younger woman replied. "We should keep our hopes up and our prayers strong."

CHAPTER TWENTY-SIX

OMA AND OPA'S HOUSE
NIJMEGEN

DIRK SAT ON THE EDGE of his bed, his face somber and his head down. "What if I never see Papa and Els again?" he said to the empty room. He lay on his back, reached into his pants pocket, and pulled out the stone from Papa.

The feel of it triggered a memory. Papa had been gone for about a month when Mama handed Dirk a small box.

"It's from Papa." Dirk opened the box and stared at the smooth, round stone inside. He looked up at Mama, confused. She smiled. "He found two stones that were almost exactly the same. He kept one and sent this one to you." She paused. "He sent an orange ribbon for Anna, and a necklace for Els."

"Is Papa all right? Where is he?"

"He's fine, and I don't know where he is. But the stone is

to remind you he loves you and he'll come back as soon as he can."

Now, lying on the bed in his grandparents' home, Dirk rubbed the stone between his fingers. The stone was to remind him of Papa. *Like he could ever forget.*

Several hours passed as he worried. Tante Cora didn't know where Papa was, Oma and Opa didn't know, and neither did the authorities. Of course they didn't know. Papa was hiding from the moffen, the masters of finding people in hiding. If Papa was hidden well enough to keep even the enemy from locating him, what chance did Dirk have of finding him? And if he couldn't find Papa, Els had no chance.

Waves of sorrow crashed against Dirk's heart, like the North Sea swells which batter the Dutch coast. He slid the stone back in his pocket and looked up at the ceiling.

"Where are you, Papa?"

Several minutes passed in silence.

Knock. Knock.

"Who is it?" he asked.

"It's Oma. May I come in?"

"Yes." Dirk sat up.

She sat next to him on the bed and put her hand on his shoulder.

"I miss your papa and Els too."

"It's not just that, Oma." He fidgeted with the stone in his pocket. "The night Mama died," he said, "she went to bed early because she was sick. I remember everything so clearly. She coughed so hard her face turned red. I asked her if I should go get a doctor, but she said no. So I made her some kwast. I mixed the last of our lemon juice with honey and hot water."

"That was a good idea," Oma said gently.

He paused again. "Papa was already gone. Els was away at university. When I got up in the morning, Mama was gone."

"That wasn't your fault." Oma squeezed his shoulder. "The doctor said your mother died of natural causes during the night."

"I know." He closed his eyes, and tears leaked out around their edges. "Oh, Oma, there's something else." He paused longer this time, taking several deep breaths. "I never told anyone this." He opened his eyes and stared at the floor. "Before I went to bed that night, I passed her bedroom." His voice quavered. "Something told me to check on her. Her door was partly open, and I reached out to push it the rest of the way." He reached his right hand out in front of him, reenacting the experience. The dam of his emotions broke open. He cried out loud, tears gushing down his face. He doubled over as his abdominal muscles forced air from his lungs so hard and so fast he could only catch quick breaths. "But for some reason," he said, still crying so hard it was difficult to speak, "I didn't open the door!" Oma embraced him, and he hugged her the way Anna had clung to him the past two months. "Don't you see, Oma? What if it's my fault? What if I had gone to get a doctor? Maybe Mama would still be alive." He continued weeping, and his right hand twitched harder than it ever had.

Oma gently pushed Dirk upright and clasped his shaking hand. "It's not your fault, Dirk. The doctor said it looked like your mother just suddenly stopped breathing. He said it probably happened so quickly that even if you had gone into her room right when she stopped breathing, you couldn't have helped her or gotten a doctor there in time."

Dirk's right hand stilled in Oma's warm grasp.

"Let me tell you something," she added. "My best friend died when I was your age."

"I didn't know that," Dirk said.

"Many people have some kind of regret after a loved one dies. I did. Having those thoughts doesn't mean it was your fault. It just means you miss your mama more than you can say."

She looked him in the eye for a long time.

"Dirk, I know what makes it all harder is that you're also worried about your papa. Don't give up on him. He's a very clever man, and Els is very strong, so don't count her out either."

She handed him a handkerchief, and he blew his nose. "A good way to lift your spirits is to help someone, and I've just the thing for you. A friend called and said the new minister is still in his office. It's dinnertime, so I made up a basket of food for him, and I want you to take it to him and visit with him. Tell him about the town and about yourself. It'll do you some good, and he might be ready for a little conversation."

Dirk nodded, and they hugged.

A few minutes later, he put on his coat and took the basket across the street. After he climbed the stone steps to the front of the church, he opened the heavy wooden front door. He walked through the foyer, opened the next door, almost as heavy as the first, and stepped into the sanctuary. It was much darker inside with only a few lights on.

When he got to the front, he made a right turn and opened a door. He entered a hallway with multiple rooms and knocked on the first door, which was partly open.

"Coming," a voice said from inside the office.

As he waited, shuffling steps inside the office approached the door. He pictured the elderly minister making his way slowly, perhaps painfully, to the door. The pastor leaned on a cane and was stooped over a bit. He looked at Dirk and the basket of food. "Ohhh. What have we here?" he said in his heavy French accent and low voice.

"My name's Dirk. My grandmother thought you might like some food."

"That is so kind. Yes, I would enjoy some food," Rev. Henri said. "Please come in." He pointed Dirk to a chair. "The food looks wonderful. And I bet you prepared it all by yourself." He winked.

Dirk blushed. "No, I only carried it here."

"Well, that's all right," he said. He handed Dirk a sandwich and kept one for himself. "I'm new here, and I've been looking forward to meeting people in town. My chance has come sooner than I thought."

"What do you mean?" Dirk asked. He set his sandwich on his lap.

"I have something important to tell you," Rev. Henri said. "But first, I want you to close the door, even though I'm pretty sure no one else is here."

Dirk's heart thudded as he rose to shut the door. "What

do you want to tell me?" he asked. *What could this man possibly know about me? Did Oma send me here for the minister to give me some bad news? Did something happen to Els?* Dirk's mouth got dry. The minister had been in a stooped position, leaning on his cane. But now he released the cane and stood up straight.

"If I tell you, you won't believe me, so I'll show you."

Dirk gripped the chair armrests tightly. The minister's French accent and low voice were gone. Dirk's mouth went dry.

Henri reached into his pocket and pulled out a gray stone, round like an extra-large coin, and held it out for Dirk to see.

Does this man have news of Papa? Did something happen to him?

Looking intently at Dirk, he said, "You have a stone that matches this one."

"Where did you get that?" Dirk asked with a shaky voice.

"I'm not a minister, I'm—"

The office door burst open, and a tall, broad-shouldered man stood in the doorway. "Hans Ingelse! You don't fool me with your beard and phony gray hair." He held a gun waist high. "Your time is up."

"No!" Dirk shouted.

"Who's the boy?" the intruder demanded. "He's your son, isn't he?"

"Leave him alone," the minister said. He stepped slowly into the center of the room, between the gunman and Dirk. "Whoever you are, your quarrel is with me."

Dirk's eyes grew wide. *It's really Papa!*

"That's fine," the tall man said with a sneer. "I'm not

interested in your son. But he's welcome to watch me destroy you."

"Who are you?" Papa asked.

Dirk looked from one man to the other, his excitement at finding Papa colliding with fear of the armed stranger.

"I am Johann Adler."

Papa pursed his lips. "Captain Johann Adler of the Gestapo, from Oosterbeek?"

The large man nodded. His big, muscular frame filled the better part of the doorway. He looked to be about thirty years old, over ninety kilograms, and his eyes gleamed with hatred. Dirk's mouth hung open. *How did this man find Papa?*

"You're the man they call the Iron Fist," Papa continued. "None of your prisoners withhold secrets because your interrogation methods are so brutal."

Adler smiled.

"Why did you hunt me down?"

"You lead the Resistance into making pathetic attempts to undermine the German authorities. You print false food ration cards to give food to Jews." He spat on the floor. Then he bared his teeth at Papa and cocked his gun.

CHAPTER TWENTY-SEVEN

DIRK'S BREATHS CAME short and fast. His palms were sweaty, and his mind raced. *No! No! You can't!*

Papa held up his hand. "I would like to say something."

"Keep it short," Adler said.

"A man with your size and strength would be unbeatable in hand-to-hand combat."

"I don't want your flattery, Ingelse!" Adler said as he took a step forward. He tapped the top of the gun barrel with his left hand.

This was way worse than when Fleischer had pulled out his gun at the ten Hakens' farm. This was Papa!

"A man like you would find more satisfaction in attacking me with his bare hands rather than using a gun."

Dirk winced and turned his head away for a moment.

"Consider the secrets you could pry out of me during torture," Papa said as he raised his hands slowly toward the ceiling.

"I don't want your secrets, Ingelse. I want your life. And

I'm going to enjoy this even more than I enjoyed tormenting your daughter, Els."

"What are you talking about?" Papa asked.

"Ohhh. So your clever Resistance friends didn't tell you we captured and tortured her," he said with a smile as thin as a knife blade.

"I don't believe you," Papa said.

"If you saw the bruises on her face and arms you'd believe me." He waved the gun back and forth. "But you'll never see her again, because— " Papa's foot flew up and knocked the gun from Adler's hand. When the weapon thudded on the floor, Adler lunged for it, but Papa kicked it under a bookshelf.

Dirk looked back and forth between the two men. He had to help Papa, but how?

Papa darted forward. When he reached Adler, Papa turned his back toward the larger man, bent at the waist, and flipped his opponent onto the floor, landing on top of him.

"Get him, Papa!" Dirk shouted.

Still on the floor, the Gestapo captain swung a left-handed punch at Papa, who leaned back out of the way, and scrambled to his feet. Adler stood and surged forward. Just before the combatants collided, Papa ducked, drove his right shoulder against his antagonist's stomach, reached down, and grasped the back of his enemy's legs below the knees. Using his low center of gravity, Papa pushed forward, briefly lifted Adler, and planted him on his back, on the floor, again landing on top of his opponent, who leaned forward and bit Papa on the arm.

"Agh!" Papa cried. He pushed away from his assailant and stood up.

"That was dirty!" Dirk roared.

Adler clambered to his feet, turned his back toward Dirk, and reached for something on the shelf in front of him. He suddenly whirled around and flung a large book at Dirk's head. Dirk raised his hands just in time to deflect the book.

"You all right?" Papa asked.

"Yes."

Adler seized the distraction to rush forward and launch a left-handed punch at Papa.

"Look out!" Dirk hollered.

Papa threw up his right hand in defense, but the blow still connected with his face. His knees buckled.

Sometimes you have to take a chance because it's the only chance you have. Dirk clenched his fists, bent at the knees and the waist, and rushed forward. *Leverage! Like Papa taught me.*

He came in low and raised his right arm to ward off blows. He quickly snaked his left arm around the back of Adler's knee, and positioned his shoulder firmly against his adversary's abdomen. He surged forward, lifted Adler's left foot a few centimeters off the ground, and pushed his enemy back toward the wall. Adler leaned forward, but that maneuver was no match for Dirk's positioning and forward momentum, which enabled him to push ahead and slam the villain into the wall.

"Ugh," Adler grunted as his back smacked the wall. Off balance, he fell and landed hard on the floor, briefly stunned by the impact.

Dirk stepped back.

"Run!" Papa shouted. They dashed out of the office and scurried down the hall into the sanctuary. Papa slammed the hallway door shut behind them and locked it. They sprinted to the back of the sanctuary, but the heavy doors that connected to the lobby were tied shut. The stout rope tying the door handles together allowed the doors to open a few centimeters, but no more.

"Can you untie it?" Dirk asked, his eyes darting back and forth between the rope and Papa.

"There isn't time," Papa said and nodded in the direction where Adler would soon emerge.

Dirk looked around wildly. "Is there a different door?"

"No. These are the only doors to the outside." Papa looked around. "Hide." He pointed toward the choir loft. "And pray."

Dirk nodded.

From far behind them, the door to the sanctuary rattled under a barrage of blows. "You can't get away, Ingelse!" their enemy yelled.

Papa dove to the floor and hid among the pews. Dirk raced to the front of the church, took the platform steps two at a time, vaulted the low wall in the front of the choir loft, and crouched out of sight. His heart raced, and it was hard to slow his breathing and listen. How could all this be happening? A few minutes ago, he had handed a sandwich to the man he thought was an elderly pastor. Since then he had found his father and used a wrestling move to take down a big, nasty Gestapo officer, and now he and Papa were in a life-and-death battle of wits with that angry and armed assassin.

The sound of something slamming into the other side of the door to the sanctuary interrupted Dirk's thoughts. Was Adler trying to kick the door open? The door rattled hard. Dirk cringed, thinking how strong Adler must be to strike the door with so much force. The third time, the door cracked, and after a few more blows, it swung open.

"Dear God, get us out of here alive," Dirk whispered.

"I know you're here, Ingelse," their pursuer growled, "and I'll find you."

Dirk chanced a quick peek over the top of the wood barrier, like an alligator whose eyes barely show above the waterline. With his back to Dirk, Adler systematically worked his way up the center aisle toward the back of the church. Holding his gun in front of him, the man looked under the pews, first left and then right. Then he advanced to the next row of pews as he worked his way back.

Dirk risked another quick glance over the wood wall. Adler was on the eighth row out of roughly fifty. At this rate, Adler would soon find Papa. Dirk swallowed hard. He had to do something, but what? His heart pounded as he glanced around the choir loft for something, anything to help Papa, but it only held chairs and songbooks. When he looked down, he caught sight of his right hand. It was calm, and he stared at it for a moment of disbelief. As he watched, his fingers grazed the outside of his pants pocket and traced the outline of the stone. Dirk clenched his jaw and then peeked again to check Adler's position. The would-be-killer was about fifteen rows from the back. *Sometimes you have to take a chance.*

Dirk gritted his teeth and pulled the stone from his pocket. He stared at it for a moment as if with a look he could communicate to the rock the urgency of its mission. Time seemed to slow down for the next few moments. Peeking out from behind the low wood wall, he gauged the distance to the back of the sanctuary. Then in one fluid motion, he rose up slightly and threw the stone high and hard toward the back-right corner of the church. He immediately lowered himself so his eyes were just above the wall. The stone clunked against a wood panel in the back of the church. Adler turned his head and rushed toward the spot. *Ha! Oldest trick in the book, and he fell for it!*

As Adler moved toward the corner, Papa made a desperate dash from the cover of the pews on the opposite side of the church, toward the hallway where he had been minutes before.

Go, Papa! Hearing footsteps, Adler whirled and fired his gun twice, but in his haste, he missed. "You can't get away!" he shouted as he rushed in hot pursuit.

Dirk ducked his head behind the wall but listened breathlessly. Adler's footsteps thundered up the aisle and toward the hallway where they had been a few minutes earlier. But that hallway didn't have another way out. What chance did Papa have now that he was trapped by Adler?

CHAPTER TWENTY-EIGHT

DE NESSE STREET
ROTTERDAM

SEVERAL HOURS EARLIER that day, a wagon carried a load of manure through Rotterdam. But it stopped on De Nesse Street. Across the street, sitting back from the window, an observer watched the driver pull the reins to halt the horses, jump down, and inspect the back left wheel. The driver was a man of average height, with a green wool hat pulled down over his ears and a black coat with the collar turned up.

With the windows of the house shut to keep out the cold, early-December air, the observer watched the driver, who complained in animated fashion, shook a gloved fist at the offending wheel, and paced back and forth for thirty seconds. He finally approached the nearest dwelling, which was a white house with bright blue shutters.

He knocked on the door, and after a long wait, a middle-aged woman answered. The watcher across the street picked up binoculars and studied the scene. The driver gestured toward the wagon and made motions with both arms in a circle about the size of a wagon wheel. The woman motioned for him to step into the house. The vigil across the street continued, with the binoculars trained on the front door.

One minute later, the door opened again, and the driver emerged with a toolbox. Across the street, the watcher set the binoculars down as the driver returned to the wagon. For several minutes, the driver pounded on the back left wheel, in what looked like an effort to reinsert a spoke into the rim. Then the driver grabbed the rim, shook it, nodded at the wheel, grabbed the tools, and headed back to the house.

The observer reached for the binoculars and watched as the driver returned the toolbox to the woman in the white house and shook her hand. The driver returned to the wagon and drove away.

Across the street, the watcher picked up the telephone. In a gravelly voice she reported, "The hen is still in her coop. Will the foxes still come to claim her in one hour?"

●　●　●

ST. STEPHEN'S CHURCH
NIJMEGEN

Hans Ingelse had dashed down the hallway, entered the fourth office down, and locked the door behind him. He scanned the room. The window was barred, so he'd have to make a stand. His adrenaline surging, he slid a heavy desk against the door with such force the telephone almost fell off the desk. Then he slid another desk behind the first one to strengthen his blockade of the door. A moment later, feet pounded down the hall in his direction. Blocking the door would delay and tire Adler. But if that monster found Dirk and turned on him, Hans would not be able to get there in time.

• • •

Adler passed the first office because the door was wide open. He stopped in front of the next office, whose door was closed. He tested the doorknob and then barged in. His eyes swept the room, but it only had a few pieces of furniture. He returned to the hall and stormed into the third office, with the same result.

"Where are you, Ingelse?" he bellowed.

He hurried to the next door. Finding it locked, he kicked hard at the door. It barely budged.

"Found you!" He glared at the door, then turned and strode into the last office he had entered, where he grabbed a meter-long metal candlestick.

• • •

Inside the office, Hans looked around. He walked to a corner of the room, grabbed a broom, and studied it. *What's Adler doing?* The office door shuddered under the force of a blow. *Won't take him long to batter down the door. Then he'll use his gun.* The door shook with another hit. Hans looked at the broom and ran his hand over the wood. But what good would a broom be against a gun? He bit his lower lip. He looked at the broom again, nodded slightly, set it down, and darted to the other side of the office. The door rattled hard. Hans grasped the edge of an oak table, and with a grunt, turned it on its side. Then he rushed back toward the desk which blocked the door. Calming himself, he did the one thing that might save his life.

When he finished, he waited while the door splintered. He held the broom handle firmly and positioned his feet shoulder width apart. He took several deep, slow breaths and prepared himself for battle. Several hard strokes later, a fist-sized hole appeared in the office door. Something clanged on the floor in the hallway. Adler's eye appeared at the hole.

Hans rammed the broom handle through the opening and it connected solidly. "Agh!" Adler roared as he pulled back from the door. "I'll break every bone in your body!"

Hans dashed to the other side of the office, taking the broom with him. He stepped over the table on its side. He knelt behind it and flattened himself on the floor.

Bullets burst through the table. Hans tapped his cheek with his finger. "You shoot like a two-year-old!" he shouted from behind the table.

More rapid-fire shots rang out, but this time only one of the bullets hit the table. Then *click, click, click.* Something clattered on the floor in the hallway. Hans pressed his lips together. *Now I just have to keep the meanest and strongest man I've ever met from finishing me with his bare hands.*

Every few seconds, the door shuddered under another blow. Over the next minute, the hole became as large as a man's head. After a brief pause, the blows resumed, and soon, the wide base of the candlestick poked through. Adler pummeled the door until the opening was big enough for his muscular torso to fit through.

• • •

Adler's chest heaved as he stuck his head and shoulders through the enlarged opening. "They said I would never get you. Said you would talk your way out of it." He crawled across the top of the two desks and stood on the floor. "My gun may be empty, but you're trapped!" With his eyes fixed on the overturned table, he slowly approached it, the way a jungle cat stalks its prey. Still a meter away from the table, he tried to peer through the bullet holes to discern where Ingelse was. Then he suddenly lunged forward and looked over the edge of the table.

Ingelse's fist shot up and caught Adler in the stomach. The younger man stepped back to steady himself. Ingelse popped up on his feet and stepped over the table. He held the broom in front of him and faced his adversary.

Adler recovered his balance and glared at his intended victim.

"I called the police," Ingelse said.

Adler pulled a knife from his boot. "My knife says you lie." He grabbed a sheet of paper from the top of the desk and easily sliced through the paper with his knife. "You're next," he said. He waved the twenty-centimeter blade back and forth.

Using both hands, Ingelse held the broom in front of him like a sword. He faked a quick stroke toward Adler's head, then in a hard swing, smashed the broom handle down on his right hand, which held the knife. The weapon fell to the floor a meter away. Ingelse rushed behind Adler, snaked an arm around his adversary's chest, thrust a leg behind him, and toppled him backward over the extended leg. Adler landed on his back with an "Oof."

As the two squared up again, Ingelse took several steps back. With the last step, he stumbled over a book that had fallen off one of the desks and landed on his back. Fueled by rage and adrenaline, Adler lunged forward and landed in a sitting position with his rear end on Ingelse's abdomen and his knees atop the fallen man's arms.

"What do you say now?" Adler gloated.

Ingelse struggled to wrench his arms free, but his younger and stronger adversary pinned them tight to the floor.

"I told you that you couldn't get away," Adler said. Ingelse tried to twist his hands free but couldn't.

"Surrender or I'll shoot!" a voice shouted in the hallway.

CHAPTER TWENTY-NINE

ADLER TURNED his head. A grim-faced Dirk held the pistol that Adler had discarded in the hall. Dirk clenched the gun in his right hand.

"The gun's empty, you stupid Dutch boy," he scowled.

"You're lying," Dirk said. He aimed the gun at the ceiling and squeezed the trigger. *Click.* He threw it at Adler but missed.

"Stay out of this or you'll be sorry!" Adler shouted at Dirk. While Adler turned his head to address Dirk, Papa wrenched one hand free momentarily.

But Adler grabbed Papa's hands and pushed them to the floor. Using his advantage of position, Adler again pinned Papa's arms beneath his knees. Adler took a few seconds to savor his triumph. As he did, Dirk clambered through the hole in the door and launched himself from the top of the desk closest to Adler and Papa. His shoulder thudded into Adler's exposed rib cage.

"Uhh," Adler grunted from the force of the impact as

Dirk knocked him off Papa, who snatched the knife from the floor, rolled away from Adler, and rose to a standing position.

But Adler grabbed Dirk around the neck in a two-arm choke hold and hoisted him to his feet. He swung Dirk around and held him in front, like a shield.

Dirk's face turned red, and his breathing became raspy. He pulled hard with both hands to release the iron grip on his windpipe, but without success.

"Let him go!" Papa said. "I'm the one you want."

"He should have stayed out of the way," Adler said, breathing hard. "Drop the knife," he hissed, reinforcing his message by increasing the pressure on Dirk's throat. Dirk groaned and tried to reach back and grab Adler's hair, but the powerful man easily avoided the flailing attempt.

"Papa," Dirk gasped. His arms fell to his sides.

Papa's face was grim as he dropped the knife at Adler's feet. "Now let him go!" Papa said.

Still behind Dirk, Adler turned to reach the knife on the floor. He released his right arm from Dirk's neck but maintained pressure with his left arm. A cold wave of fear washed over Dirk. Once Adler had the knife, he'd be in complete control. Papa must've felt he had no choice. Dirk had to try one more time. He tugged at the choke hold and tried to bite the arm pressed against his throat, but his oxygen-deprived body had little strength. His eyes bulged. His air depleted, Dirk's arms hung limp at his sides.

"Don't move," Adler warned Papa before he bent over slowly and steadily to pick up the knife. When his head was level with Papa's waist, he lunged to grasp the weapon.

At that instant, Papa swung his foot up and connected solidly with the side of Adler's head. Stunned, the Gestapo officer staggered backward and loosened his grip on Dirk's neck. The knife clattered to the floor. Dirk twisted free, stumbled forward, gasped for air, and rubbed his neck. Papa thrust a leg behind Adler and pushed him over. Before he could recover, Papa flipped him and twisted his arm behind his back.

Footsteps echoed in the hall.

"We're in here!" Papa called out. Four Dutch policemen climbed through the hole in the door and tied Adler up. They took a statement from Papa.

Adler gave Papa a steely glare. When Papa finished talking to the police, Adler said, "I'll find you again and finish you."

Papa took two steps toward the would-be assassin. He returned his stare and said firmly, "I don't think so." Then the police took Adler away.

"Dirk!" Papa clasped him in his arms.

"You beat him! You outsmarted him, Papa! And I can't believe I found you," Dirk said as they hugged. His eyes glistened.

Papa stepped back and looked at Dirk from arm's length.

"You're taller, and your voice is lower," he said. He leaned forward and grinned. "And you scared Adler, before he saw who you were. He thought you were the police." Papa chuckled.

Dirk gave a shy smile. "I was afraid my voice would crack. It still does sometimes."

Papa smiled. "It sounded like a man's voice to me."

Dirk beamed.

After a comfortable silence, Dirk shifted. "I have to tell you something."

"Go ahead."

He frowned. "I was so scared when you put the knife where Adler could reach it. Now I know why you did it. But right when it happened, I didn't understand."

"I'm sorry I frightened you, Dirk. I saw the look on your face. But I had to do it to make him let his guard down. Sometimes you have to take a chance—"

"Because it's the only chance you've got," Dirk said. Then he grinned. "You got him *good* with your foot!" He paused. "I've been trying so hard to find you, Papa, because the Gestapo took Els when we were still in Oosterbeek."

Papa's face grew pale. "So Adler wasn't lying about capturing Els." He shook his head. "When did it happen?"

"It was just before Anna and I left to go to Tante Cora's, so November 11. Can you find her and figure out a way to get her free?"

Papa narrowed his eyes. "I will do everything I can."

"I know you will, Papa." Dirk nodded a few times. "Oh, and do you know Colonel Klaus Fleischer? He's a German officer who deserted his army. He helped us get here, but I can't figure him out. When I asked him why he helped us, he wouldn't tell me, but he said you would know."

Papa's eyebrows shot up. "Klaus Fleischer helped you?"

Dirk nodded. "Do you know him?"

●　●　●

NEAR ROTTERDAM

The wagon driver with a load of manure steered onto a side road in a rural area near Rotterdam. A few minutes later, the driver directed the wagon onto a farm and into a barn with a large open door. The driver left the barn, slid the door shut, and walked to the house. An elderly man opened the door. Once inside, the driver removed the wool hat, revealing shoulder-length blonde hair.

"Els Ingelse?" the man cried. "I thought Willem was going to deliver the manure."

"We pulled one over on the Germans. Willem drove the wagon into Rotterdam and pretended it broke down in front of the house where I was staying. He put on a good show." She smiled. "He pretended to be furious with the broken wheel, and he walked up to the house to borrow tools. I was waiting inside the house, near the door, dressed just like him. After he stepped inside, I walked outside and went through the motions of fixing the wagon."

The man let out a slow whistle. "Did you have any problems?"

"Only one. He wore a green wool hat, and I couldn't walk out wearing my brown one because there were eyes on the house. So we traded hats. That's why this one is too big for me," she added with a sheepish grin.

"Were you afraid?" he asked.

She shook her head. "I was too mad at the Nazis to be afraid."

He nodded. "So you're on the run. What's next?"

"I have to get out of Rotterdam. I'll go to my oma and opa's house in Nijmegen. And then I have to find out where Dirk and Anna are."

"How will you get there?" the man objected. "I don't have a car, and I don't know anyone who does."

"Then I'll have to ride a bicycle," Els said.

"But Nijmegen's more than one hundred kilometers away!"

"Then I better get started." She reached over and patted him on the shoulder. "Keep your hopes up and your prayers strong."

CHAPTER THIRTY

ST. STEPHEN'S CHURCH
NIJMEGEN

"You know, when I was your age," Papa said, "I attended a
boarding school near the German border."

"Uh-huh," Dirk said.

Papa eased into a chair, and Dirk sat on the edge of one
of the desks.

"Fleischer and I attended the same school. He was a year
ahead of me."

Dirk's jaw dropped.

"He was the school bully, and I was his favorite target."

This news blew away any good feelings Dirk had developed
toward Fleischer, the way a hurricane wipes out a cottage.

"That's when my interest in wrestling started, because I
had to find a way to defend myself." Papa rubbed his chin.
"Klaus made my life miserable for months. Then once I got

good at wrestling, he stopped fighting me. But one day he tried a new strategy."

Lines formed on Dirk's forehead. "What happened?"

"He tried to push me in front of an oncoming train."

"What?!" Dirk shot to his feet.

"The train was some distance away, and I'm sure he only meant to scare me. He probably assumed I would have time to scramble out of the way." Papa paused. "But out of the corner of my eye, I saw him sneak up on me, and I stepped aside at the last second. He lost his balance and fell off the platform onto the track below."

Dirk scowled. "It serves him right."

"He hit his head on the rail and lay unconscious in the path of the oncoming train."

"Oh!"

"The crowd yelled at Klaus to get out of the way, and the oncoming train blasted its horn. But when Klaus didn't respond, I jumped down and pulled him out of the way."

"You saved his life!"

"He never said anything about the incident, but he never bullied me again."

"I knew it! I knew there was a good reason to not trust him." Dirk paced the room. "Do you think he helped Anna and me as a way of repaying you?"

"Yes."

"But Papa, *please* don't tell Anna why Fleischer helped us!" Dirk pleaded. "She'll bug me forever about that, since she kept telling me that he was nice. You know how Anna can be."

Papa smiled again. "It'll be our secret." He reached over and patted Dirk on the shoulder.

Dirk sat on the desk again. "I have another question. Can a dream have a warning message?"

"Why do you ask?"

"I had a dream about Mama."

Papa's smile faded.

"She warned me in a dream that I shouldn't let anyone know who I am or who you are." He looked up at the ceiling as he spoke. "In another dream, Fleischer attacked me and boasted about the eagle pin he wore. So I figured the dreams were warnings about him, but then he helped us. And a lady who tried to kidnap us wore an eagle pin just like the one in the dream with Fleischer." He lowered his gaze to meet Papa's. "So were the dreams warnings?"

"Maybe," Papa said. "You said that dream included an eagle."

"Yes."

"How good is your German?" Papa asked.

"Okay, I guess. Why?"

"The man who tried to kill me today is named 'Adler,' which is the German word for 'eagle.'"

Dirk's mouth hung open.

"Really? Wow." After a long silence, Dirk said, "I have another question. How do you still believe in God when so many bad things have happened?"

"Let me ask you a question. Why did you keep that stone I sent you?"

"It was from *you*. I held the stone sometimes when things got really bad. It meant you love us, and you'd come back to us as soon as you could. Oh, and Anna loves the ribbon you sent her."

Papa smiled. "That's how Christians are. We love the cross because it's a sign that even when things get really bad, Christ loves us and he's coming back."

"Hmm," Dirk said. "I never thought about it like that before." A brief silence followed.

Father and son talked for another hour as Dirk related the adventures and difficulties he and Anna had experienced in recent weeks.

Finally Papa checked his watch. "Oh. You'd better go back to the house. Oma and Opa will be worried. Tell them what happened and that I'm here."

"Aren't you coming with me?"

"I'll come in a few minutes. It's obviously not safe for me to be here in Nijmegen. Adler's probably not the only one who knows I'm here. Whoever sent him could send someone else after me."

Dirk took a step back. "What are you going to do?"

"I'm going to arrange to take you and Anna someplace safe. Right now I have to go to my office to gather some things that I'll need for our trip and leave notes for the other church staff."

As Papa walked down the hall to his office, Dirk went to the sanctuary, retrieved his stone, and walked across the street.

When he entered the house, Oma rushed up to him. "Are you all right?"

"Did something happen?" Opa asked.

"I'll tell you, but where's Anna? I don't want her to hear," Dirk whispered.

"She's taking a bath, and she's headed for an early bedtime. What happened to you?" Oma said with a worried look. She stabilized herself by gripping a nearby bookcase. Opa stepped closer to Dirk.

Dirk told them that the pastor was really Papa in disguise and that he would be coming over in a few minutes. Oma and Opa exclaimed in surprise. Dirk also recounted Adler's appearance and the fight, though he left out most of the details. Oma and Opa listened intently and asked a lot of questions.

Fifteen minutes into the conversation, Anna, now in her pajamas, walked into the room. She waved a finger in Dirk's face. "Where were you? You were supposed to play hide-and-go-seek with me," she said.

"He took some food to the pastor, and he stayed to talk," Opa said.

Thanks, Opa.

"And as for you, young lady," Opa said, turning his gaze toward Anna, "it's your bedtime."

"But I don't want to go to bed."

"Listen," Oma said as she led Anna toward the stairs. "Only three more days until December 5."

Anna's face lit up. "Sinterklaas!" she exclaimed.

"That's right," Oma said. "We'll leave out the wooden shoes for him. What kind of presents and treats do you think he'll bring us?"

"Ohhh!" Anna said with eyes nearly as big as stroopwafels. She threw her arms around Oma's waist and held tight.

"Now, it won't do if Sinterklaas comes and finds out you haven't been going to bed on time," Oma said as she walked up the stairs and motioned for Anna to follow. "Maybe his helper, Zwarte Piet, is listening at our chimney right now to find out if you're being good." Anna gasped, shot a look at the fireplace, and scampered up the steps. Since Dirk had been involved in Anna's bedtime routine every night for the past few months, he followed Anna up the stairs in case she asked for him.

Before lying down, she tried and failed to tie the orange ribbon in her hair.

"Let's put a rubber band around some of your pretty hair," Oma said. "Then I'll tie the ribbon in a bow, and you can pull it tight. Can you do that?"

"Uh-huh."

She turned Anna toward the mirror. Anna tugged on the ribbon, and on the third try, the bow held.

"There," Anna said. "I did it all by myself."

Oma fought back a smile.

Oma pulled the covers up to Anna's chin and patted the top blanket. She sat on the edge of the bed and closed her eyes. "Dear God, please bring Papa and Els to us. Thank you that Dirk and Anna are here. Amen."

She and Dirk walked to the door but stopped when Anna stirred.

"Oma," Anna said with a yawn, "you forgot to thank God for Sinterklaas."

CHAPTER THIRTY-ONE

TEN MINUTES AFTER Anna went to sleep, someone knocked on the front door. Oma rushed to the front of the house, Opa and Dirk close behind, and threw the door open. She looked at the bearded man on the porch and cried, "Hans!" He stepped into her embrace. Opa and Dirk joined them, and the four of them formed a hugging family circle.

"Opa and Oma," Dirk said. "I guess Sinterklaas brought our present a little early."

"Oh," Oma exclaimed. "You have to tell Anna. She's missed you so much."

"I would love to, but let her sleep for now. I'm still in danger, and I have to make arrangements to get out of the country. We'll likely leave before dawn," he said.

Oma cocked her head slightly to the side. "But Dirk said the police arrested that man who attacked you."

"Yes. But whoever sent him could send someone else."

A chill went up Dirk's spine. He tried not to think about what someone like that would do to Papa.

"May I use your telephone?" Papa asked.

"Of course," Oma said.

An hour later, Papa hung up the telephone, walked to the living room, and sat down.

"At three in the morning, someone's coming to pick up Dirk, Anna, and me. Dirk, let's wear our clothes to bed, so we can leave quickly." Turning to Oma and Opa, he said, "Soldiers will be stationed at your house around the clock to be sure that whoever's looking for me doesn't try to harm you."

Oma's eyes grew wide. "Are you sure we'll be safe? You make these enemies sound formidable."

"Yes, you'll be in good hands. I made sure of it."

"You should get Sergeant Michaels to come here. Nobody would mess with him," Dirk said.

Oma and Opa smiled.

"When our ride comes, where will we go?" Dirk asked.

"A driver will take us to Belgium, where we'll stay with friends."

"But what about Els, Papa? Shouldn't we stay here to find her?" Dirk asked.

"Once we get to Belgium, I'll make sure you and Anna are safe. Then I'll come back to find Els. But in the meantime, let's keep our hopes up and our prayers strong." He rubbed his chin. "I'll sleep in the living room tonight until I hear the signal—two quick knocks, a pause, and then a third knock. Then we'll leave, and the soldiers will come and stay here." He stood. "Get some sleep. Tomorrow will be a very good day but a long one."

Oma and Opa headed to their bedroom in the back of the house. Dirk walked up the stairs to his room.

• • •

Papa went up to Anna's room. The half moon outside gave a little light through the sheer window shade. A limp form lay on the bed, nestled under the covers.

"Oh, Anna." His voice cracked. "I've missed you so much." He stared at her face, which was the only part of her sticking out from the blankets. *My feisty Anna.* He kissed her lightly on the top of her head. He touched the orange ribbon in her hair with his fingertip and wiped his eyes with the back of his hand.

"Anna and Dirk are here, but where's Els?" he whispered. "Dear God, bring her back to us." He took a long, deep breath, exhaled slowly, and left the room.

When he reached the first floor, he walked to the living room and said to himself, "I might as well make it easier for Anna to recognize me." He walked to the bathroom and shaved his beard. Then he returned to the living room, pulled a blanket off a chair, and lay down on the floor.

• • •

At 1:45 a.m. Otto Adler rose from his recliner, walked to a nearby table, and picked up a sheet of paper with handwriting on it. He scanned the page and set it back on the table. "Johann went to kill Ingelse but didn't come back," he said to the empty room. He pounded the wall with his fist. "I bet the Dutchman outsmarted him and suckered him into talking. I told Johann not to talk! Just shoot him! But he never listens to his older brother," he growled. "I won't make that mistake."

He made a phone call.

"You ready? Good. I'll be there at 2:20." He reached for the sheet of paper. "Yes, I'm going to go over it again."

He listened.

"So that we get it done! Ingelse is a snake who slithers out of every trap. But not this one."

He was quiet for a few moments.

"No! You listen to me! We dress in black. We drive to where Ingelse is staying. He doesn't know I have eyes every-where. Ten minutes to get there. We watch the house for fifteen minutes."

He drummed his fingers on the phone table.

"At 2:45 we walk up to the house. I stand on the porch, and you crouch in the bushes, with your gun." With the phone in one hand, he shaped his other hand like a pistol.

"I knock on the door and say, 'It's Windmill. I have some-thing for you.'" He smiled. "Stupid Dutchman doesn't know I have all the code names. He sees a short man in a heavy black winter coat with hands in his coat pockets. I tell him I have an important delivery. I shake his right hand and give him an envelope with my left hand. When he looks at it, you jump on the porch. You shoot. We leave."

He was silent for thirty seconds. "Yes, I'm sure. That Jew-loving Ingelse will be dead in an hour." He hung up the phone, grabbed his notes, and fed them to the flames in the potbellied stove.

CHAPTER THIRTY-TWO

OMA AND OPA'S HOUSE
NIJMEGEN
DECEMBER 3

HANS TOSSED AND TURNED on the living room floor. He glanced at his wristwatch: *2:45.*

What was that? Footsteps on the porch? He sat up suddenly and turned toward the door. *Knock, knock.* He stood up. *Two knocks, but not a third.* His forehead furrowed. He approached the door and looked out the window. On the porch, a short man in a heavy black winter coat stood with his hands in his pockets.

"Who is it?" Hans called out through the door.

"It's Windmill," the man replied. "I have something for you."

Hans smiled and donned his coat.

When he opened the door, his breath fogged in the cold night air.

"I have an important delivery for you," the man said. He

extended his right hand for a handshake and held out an envelope with his left.

As Hans stared at the envelope, a figure clad in black rose from the bushes. The figure jumped on the porch and grabbed Hans. "Keep your hopes up and your prayers strong!"

Huh? He squinted at a few shoulder-length blonde hairs sticking out of a green wool hat.

"Papa! It's me. Els!" she exclaimed.

"Oh! Els! Oh! Oh!" Hans nearly shouted, forgetting for a moment he was outside in the middle of the night. He hugged his daughter tightly.

Recovering his wits, he said, "Quick, step into the house. We have a lot to talk about."

The man with the envelope pushed it into Hans's hand. "We scraped together a little money for your trip."

"Thank you. And thank you for bringing my daughter!" He shook the man's hand heartily. The man in the black coat melted into the darkness.

Hans and Els sat in the living room.

"Are you all right?" Hans looked at Els intently.

"I'm fine. My arms are still sore, and the bike ride was cold." She shivered.

He wrinkled his nose. "You rode a bike here? From where?"

"I started riding my bike from Rotterdam yesterday afternoon—"

"You rode all the way from Rotterdam?"

"Part of the way. I got a few rides."

"How?"

"Well, I *am* your daughter. Don't you think I've inherited some of your persuasive abilities?" she asked with a big grin. Then her smile faded. "I have to ask you, do you know if Dirk and Anna made it to Tante Cora's? I've been so worried about them." She bit her lower lip.

"Yes," he said with a smile. "But—"

The phone rang.

"Who would call in the middle of the night?" Hans said. He answered the phone, and a male voice said, "This is Wooden Shoe. After you called me, I told the police to increase their patrols near your house." He paused. "They just called."

Hans held his breath.

"They just arrested Otto Adler and an accomplice for being out after curfew."

Hans got a lump in his throat. "How close were they?"

"Two blocks from you."

Hans let out a long, slow breath. "Thank you for everything." He said goodbye and hung up.

"What was that about?" Els asked.

"Just confirmation that I'm doing the right thing by leaving," Hans said.

"Leaving? What do you mean?"

"It isn't safe for us to stay here. We're leaving in a few minutes to go to Belgium. Now you can come with us!"

"Us?" Her eyebrows shot up.

"Yes," he said. "I was starting to tell you before the phone rang that Dirk and Anna are here. Now the four of us will go to Belgium."

"They're here? I can't believe it!" She burst into a smile. "They were supposed to be at Tante Cora's. How did they get here?"

"I'll let them tell you. You'll be as proud of them as I am," he said.

A few minutes later, the conversation was still going full speed when they heard two knocks on the front door, a pause, and then a third. Hans looked out the window in the front door and saw the familiar face of a member of the Resistance. Hans invited the man in. Four soldiers came in with him to provide protection for Oma and Opa.

"It's time to go, Els," Hans said. "Go upstairs and wake your brother and sister. Dirk knows I'm here, but Anna doesn't."

Hans walked toward Oma and Opa's bedroom, but they met him in the hallway. He pointed up the stairs and said, "Listen." The three adults heard Dirk's shout of joy, followed a few moments later by Anna's squeal of delight as Els greeted them.

When they heard Els's voice upstairs, Oma and Opa shot quizzical looks at their son. He grinned from ear to ear and nodded.

"Els," Opa called. "Is that really you?"

Els dashed down the stairs and fell into her grandparents' arms. Moments later, from the top of the stairs, Anna's voice pierced through the happy reunion.

"Papa!" Anna cried. She nearly knocked Dirk over as she dashed down the stairs. She flew to her papa, and he scooped her up.

"Oh, Papa!" she said, throwing her arms around his neck.

"Anna, Anna, Anna," he said. Tears slid down his cheeks. The six family members moved into a circle of hugging.

Finally the driver cleared his throat and said, "It's time to leave."

Hans, Dirk, Anna, and Els gave Oma and Opa goodbye hugs. Hans carried Anna, who refused to let go of him, to the car. They joined Dirk in the back seat, and Els sat in front with the driver, who started the car and pulled into the dark, quiet street.

"Papa, oh, Papa," Anna sighed. "Last night I told Jesus I wanted to see you." Suddenly she drew back from him and scrunched up her nose. "But why is your hair gray?"

"It's a long story, Anna," he replied. He clutched her and stroked her hair. "I missed you so much, Anna. I missed all of you." He blew his nose.

"I missed you too, Papa," she whispered and squeezed him more tightly.

"And now I can stay with you. I'm taking you, Dirk, and Els to Belgium."

"Why?" Anna asked.

"So we can be safe."

Her eyebrows shot up. "And we'll stay together, right?"

"Yes," he said.

She burst into a big smile and hugged him hard again.

She leaned back and looked up at him. "I'm wearing the orange ribbon you sent me," she announced. She pointed to it in her hair. "I tied it on all by myself."

Hans looked at a clump of hair, tied with the orange

ribbon, sticking out at an odd angle from the side of her head. It looked like a badly rumpled sheaf of wheat in a field after a storm.

He fought back a grin. "All by yourself? It looks *beautiful.*" He hugged her again.

For the next twenty minutes or so, Els told her family about her adventures, and Dirk and Anna related theirs to her. During a brief lull in the give-and-take, Anna spoke.

"Papa, how come your clothes are like the pastor's? Is he your friend?"

Hans and Dirk exchanged smiles, and Hans's eyes twinkled.

"I guess you could say I've known him for a long time," he replied.

She snuggled into his arms and sighed. As her eyelids slowly closed, she said, "Yeah. That's what I figured."

POSTSCRIPT

THE DAY THEY LEFT Oma and Opa's house, the Ingelse family arrived safely in Belgium. The very next day, Papa bought Anna some famous Belgian chocolate.

● ● ●

Opa won election to the local municipal council, which oversaw the rebuilding of Nijmegen.

● ● ●

American officers interviewed Fleischer after he surrendered. When asked how he made it to the Allied lines to surrender, he said it was his idea to drive there. He never admitted that the suggestion came from a thirteen-year-old boy.

• • •

Els gave Dirk her heart-of-stone pebble. She described what it meant to her and added, "I want you to have it because you showed you are a lot stronger than I ever knew."

• • •

Dirk's right hand never twitched again.

ONE MAN'S PRAYER

By Hans Ingelse

I don't ask for an easy life.
An easy life for me
Means that others
Face their difficulties alone.

I do not seek praise
Because stronger people than I
Have lost their way
In the glare of acclaim.

I do not crave a soft life
Because a soft life creates a soft man
In a world that cries out for strong men.

I ask to do hard things,
For there are many hard things
To be done.

I ask you to tell me the truth,
Knowing it's better
To hear it now from a friend
Than later from an enemy.

I ask you to come with me,
Knowing that success comes
When challenges are shared,
Confidences are kept,
And friendships are honored.

I ask God
To show me how he sees me,
To give me work
That fits my talents,
And to teach me contentment
With what he provides.

If I ask
For one thing in return
It is that
When I am gone
Those who knew me best
Would say,
"He was a man
Who worked joyfully,
Gave freely,
And loved fiercely."

WHAT REALLY HAPPENED?

THE CHARACTERS IN THIS BOOK are fictional, but real historical events are woven into their story. Other events in the book are based on things that really happened, but they may not have happened exactly when or how they are described in the story. You can read about the real historical events below.

Operation Market Garden

In September of 1944, two months before this story begins, the Allies parachuted troops near the city of Arnhem, the town next to Oosterbeek (where the Ingelse family lived). The attack was a bold attempt to hasten the end of the war by dropping paratroopers behind enemy lines to gain control of key bridges over the Rhine River, or Nederrijn. The mission failed. As a result, much of the Netherlands remained under German control until May 1945.

Hunger Winter

The winter of 1944–45 became known to the Dutch as the Hongerwinter because of the scarcity of food. When the Dutch railroad workers went on strike in order to hamper German troop movements, the enemy retaliated by cutting off supplies of food and fuel to the western Netherlands, including Rotterdam. By the end of the war, the daily ration of food got down to 320 calories. That is about an eighth of the daily needs of an average adult. Things were so desperate that parents dug up tulip bulbs and cooked them. Thousands of people starved to death.

Luftwaffe Interrogations

The Gestapo used brutality to make people reveal secrets, but the Luftwaffe used kindness to get prisoners to talk. Their methods were so effective that after the war, the United States adopted these methods for their interrogations.

Razzias

Late in the war, the occupying Germans swept through towns in the Netherlands, kidnapping adults and teenagers and forcing them to work in German factories.

Anna's Orange Ribbon

Orange has patriotic significance for the Netherlands because the Dutch royal family is known as the House of Orange. Dutch patriotic radio broadcasts from England back to the

Netherlands were known as Radio Oranje. Erik Hazelhoff Roelfzema, the Netherlands' most heroic Resistance fighter, was known as the Soldier of Orange.

Dutch Bicycles

The story makes mention of the Dutch riding and loving their bicycles. The Germans confiscated many bicycles during the occupation but didn't get them all. When the Germans increased their bicycle thefts, the Dutch hid their bikes. I interviewed one family who buried their bike to keep the Nazis from getting it.

St. Stephen's Church

There really is a St. Stephen's Church in Nijmegen. It was badly damaged during an Allied bombing attack in February of 1944.

AN INTERVIEW WITH DR. CURRIE

How long did it take you to write *Hunger Winter*?
It took seven years.

Where did you get the idea for the book?
Three things influenced me. First, I have had a lifelong interest in World War II and the Holocaust because my father was a World War II veteran. Second, my wife is of Dutch heritage. The third influence came when my son Steven, who was a seventh grader at the time, wrote a short story set in the Netherlands during the war. I thought it would be fun to develop that story into a book.

How much of what's in *Hunger Winter* is historically accurate?
The characters are fictional, but the vast majority of what they do is based on actual events.

What kids' books do you like?
My favorites include A Day No Pigs Would Die, Gregor the Overlander, *and* Snow Treasure.

What are your favorite World War II movies?

I like The Hiding Place *and* Return to the Hiding Place, *which are both about World War II in the Netherlands.*

Where did you get ideas for your characters?

Dirk is a combination of the many boys I have known and worked with in a variety of contexts. Colonel Fleischer was loosely modeled after Long John Silver in Treasure Island *because I found him to be an interesting character.*

As you did research for your book, what surprised you the most?

I was stunned at the Luftwaffe's method of interrogation, which was just as portrayed in this story. They used kindness as a key element of getting secrets from prisoners of war. Several captured Allied pilots remained friends with their Luftwaffe interrogators after World War II, and the US military was so impressed, it adopted many of the Luftwaffe's methods after the war.

How does the timeline of Anne Frank's story compare with the events of this book?

Anne was captured on August 4, 1944. This story begins in November of 1944.

DISCUSSION QUESTIONS

A Note to Teachers: Please visit www.robcurrieauthor.com for many additional teaching resources, which include links to YouTube videos and much more.

1. Which character in the story showed the most bravery? Explain your choice.

2. As you read this book, what surprised you the most about the Dutch experience during World War II?

3. What was the most important thing Dirk learned from Papa?

4. If you could ask one character in the book a question, who would it be and what would you ask him or her?

5. Who changed more, Dirk or Els? Explain your choice.

6. How would the story have been different if Mama hadn't died?

7. Dirk and Els both cherished a stone. Were their reasons similar or different?

8. What was Anna's best personality trait?

9. Pick a character from the book, and choose three words to describe his or her personality.

10. Did Dirk's responsibility to take care of Anna change him? If so, how did he change?

11. Would you advise Hans Ingelse to stay safely in Belgium or to return to the Netherlands to help the Resistance? Why?

12. Imagine that you and your family are helping the Resistance and your best friend's parents are collaborators. Could you still be good friends with that person? Why or why not?

13. If you had lived during the war, how willing would you be to risk your safety to protect people you don't know?

14. If you suddenly had to flee your home to be safe from the Nazis and you could pack only one bag, what would you put in it and why?

15. Dirk talked about taking a chance when it's the only chance you've got. How do you know whether it's a good idea to take a chance?

16. What kind of further adventures do you think Dirk might have in his future?

17. The characters reminded each other to keep their hopes up and their prayers strong. How did a positive attitude help them? How does a positive attitude help you?

18. Pick a favorite character from the book. If this book were made into a movie, which actor or actress would you like to see portray that character? Explain your choice.

19. Dirk was inspired by his papa's advice and encouragement. Who has inspired you, and how did that person do it?

20. Pick a character in the book, and explain how that person is similar to you and in what ways he or she differs from you.

KEY WORLD WAR II DATES
FOR THE NETHERLANDS

September 1939	Britain and France declare war on Germany, while the Dutch proclaim neutrality.
May 10, 1940	The Nazi army attacks the Netherlands.
May 14, 1940	The Luftwaffe destroys central Rotterdam by bombing.
May 15, 1940	The Netherlands surrenders to Germany.
February 25–26, 1941	Protesting Jewish deportations, thousands of Dutch workers go on strike.
April 29, 1942	The Nazis force all Jews to wear a yellow star identification badge.
July 6, 1942	In Amsterdam, Anne Frank and her family conceal themselves in a secret apartment.

June 6, 1944	The Allies invade German-held France on what we call D-Day.
August 4, 1944	The Germans arrest Anne Frank and her family.
September 5, 1944	Many Dutch people believe rumors that their country is about to be liberated. Dutch patriots celebrate Dolle Dinsdag, or Mad Tuesday, and many collaborators move to Germany to escape repercussions.
September 14, 1944	The Allies push back the German occupation, freeing the first Dutch cities.
September 17–25, 1944	Operation Market Garden, a bold Allied surprise attack at the border of the Netherlands and Germany, attempts to hasten the end of the war but fails.
September 1944	Thousands of Dutch train workers go on strike to hinder German troop movements. Angered by the strike, the Nazis cut off food and fuel to the occupied Netherlands.

September 1944– May 5, 1945	Thousands of Dutch civilians starve or freeze to death during what they call the Hongerwinter.
May 5, 1945	The Netherlands is liberated from German occupation.

ACKNOWLEDGMENTS

SPECIAL THANKS go to my literary agents, Bob Hostetler and Les Stobbe, and to my editor, Sarah Rubio, as well as my writing friends Randy Gauger, Pat Hargis, Dean Hufsey, Gabriele Pflaum, Shaina Read, Janet Riehecky, and Tim Shoemaker, and the Write-to-Publish Writers' Conference for their advice and encouragement which made this book possible.

ABOUT THE AUTHOR

RAISED IN THE SUBURBS of Detroit, **Rob Currie** majored in psychology at Cornerstone University before earning his master's and doctorate degrees in psychology at Saint Louis University. He met and married his wife in Saint Louis.

An avid reader, Rob's favorite books are about World War II. His veteran father cultivated this interest by frequently sharing stories of bravery and ingenuity which contributed to the Allied victory. Other interests include cooking, playing basketball, and writing whimsical poetry.

Rob has taught psychology at Judson University since 1987. In 2001 he published *Hungry for More of God*. He published *Preschool Wisdom: What Preschoolers Desperately Want to Tell Parents and Grandparents* in 2011.

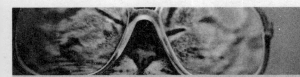

FOR ADVENTURERS

The Wormling series

Red Rock Mysteries series

FOR COMEDIANS

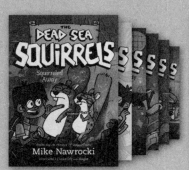

The Dead Sea Squirrels series

FOR ARTISTS

Made to Create with All My
Heart and Soul

Be Bold

FOR ANIMAL LOVERS

Winnie the Horse Gentler series

Starlight Animal Rescue series

IT'S LIKE CAPTAIN UNDERPANTS MEETS THE BIBLE, BUT REVERENT!

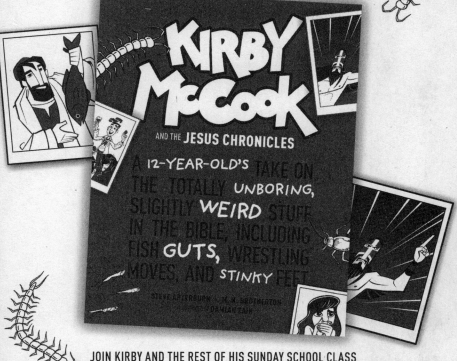

JOIN KIRBY AND THE REST OF HIS SUNDAY SCHOOL CLASS AS THEY TAKE A WILD JOURNEY THROUGH THE BIBLE AND LEARN THAT JESUS IS AT THE CENTER OF THE STORY.

THAT'S ME, KIRBY